The Last Night of a Damned Soul

The Last Night of a Damned Soul

A NOVEL BY

SLIMANE BENAÏSSA

Translated from the French by

JANICE AND DANIEL GROSS

Grove Press
New York

Originally published in 2003 in French under the title *La dernière nuit d'un damné*
by Editions Plon, Paris.

Published simultaneously in Canada
Printed in the United States of America

FIRST EDITION

Library of Congress Cataloging-in-Publication Data
Benaïssa, Slimane.
    [Dernière nuit d'un damné. English]
    The last night of a damned soul / by Slimane Benaïssa ; translated by
Janice and Daniel Gross.
        p. cm.
    ISBN 0-8021-1780-5
    1. Gross, Janice.   II. Gross, Daniel.   III. Title.
PQ3989.2.B388D4713 2004
843'.914—dc22   2004052376

Grove Press
841 Broadway
New York, NY 10003

04 05 06 07 08   10 9 8 7 6 5 4 3 2 1

To my brother Mohamed, whom I miss dearly.

To my mother . . . who would say:
—I hope to be gone before you; if you were to die before
me, my grief would be unbearable . . .
—Even if I die as a hero?
—You would be a hero for those who pushed you into
death, not to the woman who brought you into life.

Author's Foreword

In 1832, Victor Hugo wrote *The Last Day of a Condemned Man*. As a result of the French Revolution and the Rights of Man, the death penalty was abolished. Hugo was its instigator.

In 1962, Solzhenitsyn wrote *One Day in the Life of Ivan Denisovitch* as a plea against the slow death in the gulags of peoples' revolutions, and against all walls, which ultimately led to the fall of the Wall.

I feel connected to both of these writers, first because they are my literary masters, but especially because of the present historical context. As in their case, I feel that history forces me to speak out responsibly against certain unjust, inadmissible, and inconceivable deaths. My response as a Muslim is dictated by my personal experience with religious extremism, which forces me to speak out, and, like Tom Thumb, to place the third stone in the way of ogres in order to point the way toward humanity. By writing *The Last Night of a Damned Soul*, I hope to put forth a plea against all ideologies of death.

There are certainly thousands of ways to live as a Muslim. Unfortunately, in today's world there seem to be only two: one is an Islam that is expressed through all manner of violence, the other is an Islam that is silent and whose silence amounts to more than just an absence of words.

As for me, if I were a contemporary of the Prophet Muhammad and I heard him say: "Turn your children into bombs for the glory of God," I would not have embraced Islam.

Maybe by saying that, I'm no longer considered Muslim. But what does it matter?

The most important thing is not to admit, for whatever reason, that the death of the young can become engraved in the memory of Islam in today's world and for generations to come. How could anyone think that one can believe in a God that would take pride in such deaths? To do battle in the name of God is to think first of God, and not of the enemy.

I know that there is much suffering in the world. Powerful governments, poverty-stricken peoples, globalization at every turn, economics taking precedence over humanity, etc. . . . The solution to all of these problems, admittedly significant, is, in my mind, to be found outside of the realm of religion.

Besides, with the "death of ideology," it is clear that a single system now dominates and no one can avoid it. And when we hear that "there is no more history," it's because there is only one kind left: the one that acts while the majority of others follow. It shouldn't be surprising, then, that religions are becoming more political as a way to fill a vacuum and construct, each in their own way, an opposing position.

The Last Night of a Damned Soul is fictional in the sense that I am not to be found in any of the characters, nor are they real. They are certainly my inventions, but only so that they can be what they are. After September 11, I asked myself the same question every other human being asked: how was it possible? If it was carried out, then it's because, from a technical point of view, it was feasible. If the CIA and the FBI were outmaneuvered, it's because they were ripe for being outmaneuvered. But the terrible question remains: how was it possible from a psychological, religious, and spiritual point of view? This is the question I have tried to answer from my perspective as an Arab and a Muslim by recounting the three-year period leading up to the attack in an attempt to explain the possibility of this impossibility.

Speaking as a Muslim, I ask for forgiveness from all of the families who have been victims of religious extremism across the globe, regardless of their faith.

I also ask them for forgiveness regarding some of the harsh sections in this novel. Throughout the entire time of writing, I wondered whether I should say what I felt to be the most illuminating truth, or take into consideration the pain it might bring to the victims' families. In this situation, more than in any other, truth is painful but it must be confronted out of respect for the victims, for those who died, and there is no greater pain than to describe hatred when it is expressed in the name of the religion of my mother, of my father, and of my sheikh and spiritual guide, the very ones who are peace itself in my eyes.

S.B.
Massy, March 27, 2002

Publisher's Note

To help the reader follow more easily, each form of religious writing is presented in a distinct way. Quotations from the Koran are shown centered, with the first word of the quotation in small capital letters; they are also followed by citations of which sura and verse of the Koran they are drawn from, abbreviated S and V. The words of the Prophet or the Hadith are italicized and the other prayers are inset and in smaller type.

At the end of the text, the author has provided a glossary of the Arabic terms used.

Translators' Notes

To demonstrate how Islamic teachings were used to shape the thinking of the main character Raouf, Slimane Benaïssa's novel makes use of extensive quotations from three types of religious writing. As a Muslim trained to read the Koran in its original Arabic, the author translated his reading of the Koran into French. It is important to note that the Koran in Arabic is considered to be the sacred and direct word of God as revealed to the Prophet Muhammad through the archangel Gabriel. In any other form, the text is a translation and is viewed as an interpretation of the original. The English translations in this novel are all based on the French as rendered by the author from the original Arabic. Quotations of the Koran are identified by sura and verse. We would like to thank Michael Sells for his suggestion that we translate the Koran passages directly from the author's original French. His penetrating study and select translations in *Approaching the Qur'an*, further informed our understanding of the expressive quality of oral recitation techniques of the Koran in Arabic.

The second form of religious writing is taken from the Sunna (actions and sayings of the Prophet Muhammad) as contained in the Hadith (sayings of the Prophet). The complexity of this material poses challenges for translators and readers alike. The secondary material of the Sunna and Hadith is printed in italics, while the numerous prayers and supplications are inset. The author provides two glossaries at the end: one of Arabic terms, the other of historical figures in Islam. While the transliteration of Arabic terms into English produces a variety of spellings, we have tried to select those that would be most familiar to the general reader. The five chapters of the novel represent the five daily prayer times required of all Muslims. These prayers or *salat* constitute one of the Five Pillars of Islam.

We would especially like to thank the author for bringing us to this project, and for his generous help in clarifying certain terms and unfamiliar references. We acknowledge his courage in turning to the novel as a way of introducing complex perspectives on Islam to a broad reading public, both Muslim and non-Muslim. While this approach is admirable, it is not without obvious risks. Yet, as Slimane Benaïssa is quick to point out, the alternative of silence is, by far, the greatest risk. It is our deepest hope that we have done justice to his desire to make this important work accessible to an English-speaking public.

Our thanks go to François Massonnat, whose sensitivity and talent in both French and English helped to inform the final translation, and to Amy Hundley at Grove Press for her insights and care throughout the editing process.

Janice and Daniel Gross

I

It was *Eid al-Adha,* the Feast of the Sacrifice, during the third weekend of May. Athman picked me up at dawn to drive a few miles out of town to a ranch owned by a Saudi emir for the sacrifice of the lamb. I was doubly excited about this outing. On such a glorious day, I looked forward to reliving memories of the vacations I used to spend with my grandparents in Lebanon. And I was looking forward to letting my black Lab, Keytal, feast on the treat of fresh meat.

As Athman honked the horn, Keytal bounded toward the door, as if sensing the pleasures that awaited him. He twitched in anticipation and leaned his snout on the doorknob while I gave a quick hug to my girlfriend Jenny, who was sulking about not being invited simply because she was a woman. She was annoyed because she couldn't understand how I could agree with such intolerance, although, as I tried to explain, "It's not intolerance. These are just restrictions of the religion, that's all."

She held in her tears, I held back a kiss, and got in the elevator with the excited Keytal. As soon as Athman saw my dog, he jumped out of his car, furious.

"Oh no! No dogs!"

"Why is that a problem?"

"In the eyes of Islam, dogs are the dirtiest of animals. If they touch you, you have to redo your ritual cleansing. What's worse is that he's black. The Prophet said, 'A black dog is a *shaytan*.' No, no, no . . . there's no way I'll have him in my car."

Athman was so upset that I had no choice but to take the dog back up to Jenny, who couldn't make sense of this sudden change of plan. Not wanting to give the real reason, I was forced to lie to her for the first time in our relationship.

"The dog's too wired."

"What do you mean? He seems normal to me."

"He's really pretty excited, can't you tell? He's even getting aggressive."

"Maybe he's excited, but he's not wired."

She took the animal in her arms and began to pet him. Keytal gave me a pathetic and accusatory look. He was sad because he knew that he would be left behind in the apartment. It pained me to do that. I could tell Jenny wasn't happy either. She didn't understand my reaction and looked very worried. I ended up admitting the truth.

"In Islam, dogs, especially black dogs, are not allowed."

"Are you kidding? If I were you, I'd watch out for people who discriminate against dogs and women. That leaves out a lot of people for a so-called celebration."

Jenny pulled Keytal inside and slammed the door in my face, leaving me stuck on the landing.

I had hardly gotten into the car when Athman instructed me to turn off my cell phone, take off my watch, my chain, and my ring, and put them all in the glove compartment. Then he said, "You have to turn off the cell phone for security reasons. If there's a cell phone turned on anywhere, all your movements are recorded. As for the jewelry, there are religious reasons. God doesn't like men who adorn themselves, especially in silk and gold. From now on, no more jewelry. As for the watch, you'll have only one time from now on: the one that God decides for you. So, buckle up and we're off!"

"I really would like to stop by my mother's for breakfast."

"Does she know about it?"

"Yeah! Surely you don't expect me not to stop by to wish her a happy *Eid*."

"No, I mean does she know that I'm coming with you?"

"Sure. And if you wouldn't mind, as soon as you see a florist, I'd like to stop to pick up some flowers for her."

"You buy flowers for your mother?"

"Of course! It's a special holiday."

"But flowers aren't part of our tradition. Bringing flowers to my mother would never cross my mind."

"Why not?"

"Because we only give gifts that nourish, not ones that perish."

"My mother has a Western side to her, she loves flowers. She wasn't born in a desert you know."

"You cater to your mother's Western side and you neglect her Muslim side during an Islamic feast?"

"What can I say? If you see a Middle Eastern pastry shop near the florist, stop and I'll buy her some fine baklava as well."

"I know a good place with just the right gifts not too far from the florist. . . ."

At the stoplight Athman took a right toward the Muslim neighborhood. He talked me into buying prayer beads, some henna, and musk incense for my mother.

"You must be crazy," I said, "she hates the smell of musk; it reminds her too much of death."

"But she's mortal like all of us! She ought to get used to the idea because death is inevitable."

I bought my three usual roses: a red one, a white one, and a yellow one. Then we headed for the shops adjacent to where my mother lives. My parents bought a two-bedroom condominium in a luxury development situated next door to the neighborhood shops where my mother does her shopping. It makes her feel right at home.

Athman hesitated and then asked me, "Why not buy roses of the same color?"

"The red one stands for my mother, the white one for me, and the yellow one for my father."

"A rosy family of sorts . . . do you know what those colors mean in Islam?"

"No."

"Red is for blood, white is for the shroud, and yellow is for hypocrisy."

"You don't know how true that is. . . ."

✼   ✼   ✼

My mother was waiting for us, with her Lebanese elegance, which was less the result of trying to look beautiful than of wishing to maintain a timeless beauty that would change little, no matter the circumstance. She has a way of dressing and wearing makeup that makes her seem ageless, so that whenever we pulled out the old photo albums during family gatherings, our favorite game was to try to guess the date of photos which contained my mother. With a little luck, we could guess within five years.

My mother met us at the door, placed her hands on my cheeks, and kissed me. She was pleased and touched that I brought her the three roses. As I handed her the other gifts, I said in a low voice: "These are from Athman."

Then she led us into the living room where she had set a magnificent table with traditional Lebanese pastries, as she invited us to sit down.

"You know, my son, ever since I've been here, the Muslim feasts seem dull because we're far from our native land. When the Christian holidays come, we celebrate them more out of imitation than conviction. Our life is a series of empty gestures which are not really sins, because our sense of responsibility toward our distant homeland and our lack of connection to life here is unclear."

In reality, I thought my mother was just trying to find a way to rationalize the fact that this was the first *Eid al-Adha* she had to celebrate without my father. My father was a design engineer in medical electronics who specialized in chemotherapy products. He had been stricken by leukemia, and died within a span of just a few weeks. My mother remained convinced that he died of accidental and prolonged exposure to X-rays, but she had not yet managed to prove it after ten months of investigation. Despite an autopsy and technical reports, the company would only acknowledge the possibility of a work-related illness, but soundly rejected the theory of an actual work-place accident. We waited well over a week for the return of his remains. Not knowing exactly how he died or where he would be buried, my mother, lost in confusion and grief, muttered, "We never knew how to give meaning to our joy, and now we don't know how to make sense of our sorrow. It's so unfair."

As for me, I missed my father terribly. He was so much a part of my very being that his love bonded me to eternity. Each time I tried to get used to the idea of his death, I felt dizzy, I could barely stand up, I was weakened by a desire so strong that it pushed me to join him beyond death, wherever he was.

As long as our parents are alive, we have the impression of being sheltered from death as if they constitute a protective wall. When my father died, I felt thrust into the front row, into the line of fire. At that moment my protective armor fell off and a flood of existential questions overwhelmed me, leaving me fragile and vulnerable. I would feel my mind go blank, and I began having knots in my stomach, and bouts of insomnia. . . . All of these previously unknown ailments came together. I couldn't concentrate at work and I had lost interest in my life. Time and space no longer had the same dimensions. It was as if my biological clocks had stopped functioning properly. Life and death no longer had the same meaning. I had to wonder whether I ever really understood it all before. My father had been a kind of ozone layer that rested above my world. Since his death, I feel cold, less alive. He was a big, strong man who combined a scientist's brain with an artist's heart. When he helped me with my homework, he would talk about physics and math as if they were stories, making equations and numbers come alive. And when he played the lute on my birthdays, I felt myself growing taller. His lute now lies silent in the display case in the living room. Imbued with so much celebration, it asks each passerby in the house to explain the absence of the musician.

My mother was so wrapped up in her own suffering that she couldn't help me at all with mine. We couldn't come together to share our pain. Each of us was afraid of talking out of fear of hurting the other. In this space where the terror of the unspoken paralyzed us, we tried to go on living together. This pain that seemingly nothing could transcend, not reading, nor films, nor work, nor alcohol, was like a constant flatline superimposed over the regular rhythm of a normal electrocardiogram. Life seemed to be increasingly empty and painful, and I struggled to fill it. For me, time no longer had the same duration. It was short when I thought of death, long when I thought of life, fear appeared on one side, ennui on the other. In the turmoil of mounting grief, I became aware of my own ignorance, and in spite of all my years of study, I couldn't get beyond this fear, and in spite of all my cultural awareness, I was mired in ennui. I existed on a fault line that I carried within me. I couldn't escape without pulling myself apart in the process.

My mother interrupted my reverie by knocking over a cup; she wouldn't dream of just asking me what was on my mind.

"Oh, I'm so sorry. I don't know where my head is these days."

She rushed to the kitchen to get something to clean up the mess. Athman gave me a sharp nudge with his elbow and said, "Please talk to your mother. I have no idea what to say to her."

She returned with a sponge and a question: "Where will the sacrifice of the lamb be performed?"

"At Jamal's. He's a friend of Athman, a prince from Kuwait."

"You mean *the* Prince Jamal himself?"

Athman interjected, "It will be held at the house of a Saudi friend of Jamal's. We're going as Jamal's guests."

Surprised, I asked my mother, "You know Prince Jamal?"

"Only by reputation, nothing more. This is a royal *Eïd*, if I understand correctly."

"It's more communal, since it brings several families together."

"It still could be a royal community."

"If you want, you can come with us."

"You very well know, my son, that since your father's death we're not a family any longer."

Very politely and even timidly, Athman thanked my mother, and apologized for our having to leave because we had to be on time for prayers. My mother didn't press it. She saw us to the door and said to me: "Don't forget! Tomorrow I'll be waiting for you so we can go visit your father."

"I'll be there at one. See you tomorrow."

The two-lane road that runs through the city for several miles reveals the changes in real estate for the last century or so. At the eleventh stoplight on the right a small road continues and crosses a cornfield, and at the end of the road is the oldest farm in the region, which still bears the name of its founder, Peter Ferguson. His heirs refused to sell off the property. They stood up to developers and politicians alike, even during the years of the worst harvests when they could barely make their monthly payments. And now these same promoters and politicians are grateful to them for keeping open this "window" of nature in the midst of an endless expanse of concrete. For the view, drivers would try to get stuck at the red light, which played right into the hands of the greedy admen and politicians because the eleventh light is peppered with billboards claiming this swath of natural countryside "courtesy of such-and-such a brand or party." In point of fact, this farm is the laboratory where my mother works as a biologist specializing in genetically modified grain.

Athman and I work just beyond this "paradise." For over a year now, we've gone by this place on our way back and forth to work. This landscape gives a lift to Athman's good moods and helps him breathe easier when he's down. Trapped between two glass-fronted apartment buildings, this countryside looks as unreal as a primitive art painting. For Athman, who was taught that logic is always contained within its own closed system, this paradise is proof that one can question logic regardless of the system that protects it.

A mental puzzle like this appeals to computer technicians and software developers like Athman. He likes to say that by destroying logic, a new structure of meaning could result, and that those new meanings could undermine the logical structure on which they are based.

This window of paradise has a meaning that makes sense to him. When he is stopped at the red light, he clicks on his imagination, escapes within himself, and sinks into a silent recitation of verses from the Koran.

Besides his reading of the Koran, Athman reads three books a week: one in Arabic, one in French, and one in English. He doesn't like films, sports or TV, and bars aren't his scene. He has only two passions: Islam and reading. As he says, "The first word God said to Muhammad was 'Read in the name of God.' Reading is therefore God's commandment. Q.E.D.

He doesn't drink, he doesn't smoke, he eats little and leaves the table still a bit hungry as the Prophet's tradition recommends. His day begins with sunrise prayers, then he goes running in the neighborhood. After twenty minutes of jogging, he buys some cold milk and a croissant. When I told him that the croissant wasn't very Muslim, he protested:

"You see, you don't even know your own history. The croissant and all other kinds of flaky pastry are Turkish. The Europeans got to know them only thanks to the Ottomans and the croissant was originally rolled out straight. One day a Viennese pastry chef decided to shape it into a crescent to let everyone know that the Turks were encircling the city."

After his shower and breakfast of Turkish croissants, he gets dressed for work. His wardrobe consists of five suits for work, which he calls his "disguises" for the Here and Now. He wears only the big name designers. He says that they give him the most comfortable fit because designer clothes are always well made, and he can pass unnoticed because the best way to remain anonymous is to dress in style. He also has three Islamic outfits for mosque and home. These are his "faith clothes."

Athman was born in Nazareth. He's Palestinian by birth but has Jordanian nationality. After his secondary studies in Amman, he joined an uncle living in Strasbourg where he did advanced computer studies. As soon as he'd defended his doctorate brilliantly, he was recruited by one of the biggest German computer firms in Berlin thanks to a network of his uncle's friends. It was this German company that sent him off to Silicon Valley six months later.

Three years later, he landed the job with the company where I work, and ever since, we've shared the same office. When our eyes get red and LCDed out, we take a coffee break and Athman decompresses by talking about his life: "Last year in Silicon Valley was a real pain for me. You get all these young guys coming from all corners of the world to make a killing in a few months which makes for some insufferable ego trips. These guys are spiritually handicapped, their language isn't made up of letters, words, or sentences anymore, but out of mathematical assertions, computerized structures, and money. Their houses become their consecrated temples and their cars, the beacon of their blazing success. These are people who, every day, translate what they're told into computerese to better understand it. By immersing themselves in the computer's logical universe, their poetic sensibility is reduced to less than nothing. Often, when you quote them a poem, they answer: 'Which web site do I have to click on to get it?' Their favorite slogan is "I think, therefore I am" is ancient history; "I click therefore I solve" is the future.

"At twenty-nine years of age they're CEOs of companies in a modern Babylon. They play the market with millions of jobs and the stocks of thousands of retired small investors, and when the whole thing hits the fan, they get well paid to move on."

It was during our daily commute to work that Athman would talk to me about God, the Prophets, and the Prophet Muhammad. We rarely talked about problems at work because we barely had any. Since we were both researchers and software developers, we had total independence in the company, so if we could figure something out, so much the better, and if we couldn't, we were doing research all the same.

This was the first time I made the trip with Athman when we weren't going to work. Once we passed the cornfield light and my mother's paradise, Athman tried to make amends for the thing with my dog: "Hindus venerate cows. As for us, we hate dogs, while the Chinese eat them. All religions define very specific relationships with animals. You have to be aware of them, that's all. That's why if you are prepared to repent and receive God, you've got to get rid of your dog."

"But Keytal is housebroken, he has all his shots, and he's a human-like dog, or a dog-like human, whatever."

"Only God is capable of changing the nature of things. A dog is a dog. Period. If you lived in a house, the dog would have his own special spot outside the front door and wouldn't come in to your living space. But you live in an apartment and the dog sleeps next to you in your bed and he has free rein. Your place isn't so much an apartment as a satanic dog den."

He burst out laughing happy with his invention. I reminded him, "It's not my place, but Jenny's."

"What's the difference? It's where you live. You'll have to get rid of it. The Prophet puts it this way: '*When you hear dogs barking at night, ask God for refuge from them, for they can see what you cannot.*'"

Then he went back to being serious saying, "After all, it's very appropriate to talk about the place of animals in Islam on the day of *Eid al-Adha* when we prepare to sacrifice a lamb to honor Abraham's patience and Ishmael's submission and not Isaac's, like for the Jews. They celebrate Passover, which is a kind of *Eid al-Adha* for them."

"You mean the opposite."

"What do you mean?"

"Since the Jewish religion comes before Islam, it should be that *Eid al-Adha* is a kind of Passover for Muslims. A father never looks like his son, it's the son who looks like his father."

"This is exactly where the great theological errors begin. Physical and material resemblances don't work in the same way as spiritual resemblances. It's the rough draft that always precedes the final copy. And what makes the rough draft what it is? It's the final clean copy. You always have the rough draft in the final copy. That's why all religions of the Book are read in relation to Islam, because it's God's last message and final copy to humanity. As for Islam, it's read only in relation to God. So as I was saying, Passover is a kind of *Eid al-Adha* for the Jews with one big difference: for them, Abraham received the order to sacrifice Isaac. That's where you can see the falsifications of the Jews. Abraham had a son, Ishmael, with Hagar, a slave brought back from Egypt, because Abraham's wife, Sarah, couldn't have children. Sarah, who had problems accepting the situation even though she considered Ishmael her son, was fiercely jealous of Hagar. Abraham loved Sarah very much and couldn't stand to see her so unhappy. Every night he prayed to God to make Sarah pregnant. But God had to put Abraham to the test before answering his prayers. He asked him to sacrifice his son Ishmael and because Abraham obeyed and Ishmael submitted, Sarah got pregnant with Isaac. The Hebraic religion was born because Ishmael showed submission to God, that is to say, he underwent 'Islamization.' Jews exist thanks to Islam and not the other way around. That's how it is in theology: what appears to be one thing is actually another. Ishmael, in submitting to God's order, became a Prophet with the charisma befitting the Prophets. When Isaac came into the world, Ishmael had influence over him, which Sarah didn't like. That's what made her tell Abraham to chase out Hagar and her son. The exile that Sarah inflicted on Ishmael and his mother would become an eternal exile for the Jews. Anyway, their return to Israel was only a respite before other exiles. In order to tell us apart from each other, God decreed that the Jew is a Jew through the mother, and the Muslim is Muslim by the father. That's why there are ten million of them scattered throughout the world and two billion of us. We're the authentic sons of Abraham while they are only Sarah's sons. . . ."

Athman's reasoning left me feeling confused. One of two things must be going on: either he knew too much or he didn't know enough, because he would use shortcuts which astounded me. In the case of his knowing too much, his reasoning was the result of true erudition and if so, I would learn something. If he didn't know enough, that meant he would appropriate any event to fit into his own logic. In this case, that would make him a propagandist.

What bothered me was that I couldn't find ways to challenge his arguments, so I submitted to them.

"Do you know where the word Israel came from?" And then he was off again. . . .

"No, I don't know."

"When Jacob fought with God, he was baptized Israel because to fight in Hebrew is *izra,* and God, *El.* Together that makes: Izra-El. God broke one of Jacob's hips so that he would remember this struggle. Because of it, Jews never eat leg of lamb without removing the sciatic nerve. And today they are making the same mistake because they are fighting against our God, and they're going to end up with the other hip broken!"

Athman burst out laughing, pleased with his rendition. What made me uneasy around Athman was his grating and violent political humor, which didn't recognize even the freedom of laughter, because if you laughed, that meant you agreed with him. He didn't understand that you could laugh just at the quip and not necessarily at the idea itself.

Athman had a golden brown complexion, a gaunt profile, and thick black hair that he cut very short. His wide irises
dominated his eyes and deepened his gaze, compounding its
severity. Fortunately, his shining white smile was outlined
by fleshy lips. He had the beauty of a woman and the faith
of a man. Tall and thin, Athman was exceptionally elegant,
the result of Islamic reserve and religious conviction. In addition, he was athletic-looking without being muscle-bound.
He could have played a magnificent biblical character in one
of those 1950s film epics. When he passed by, women would
be swept away in his wake. He would make fun of their sap-
piness and scorn their admiration. He was adamantly intol-
erant when it came to being too close to women. He shook
their hands only as a strategic cover-up, and if he could avoid
it, he would.

A male model type who saw himself as a "high mullah,"
Athman was married to an eighteen-year-old Moroccan taxi
driver's daughter. His wife still lived with her parents to help
take care of her mother, who'd been blinded in an accident
with some harsh cleaning chemicals. Athman visited his wife
once a week. The rest of the time he lived alone in his studio apartment because he considered himself to be in a state
of *jihad* and men in combat were supposed to have as little
to do with women as possible.

There were two Arabic inscriptions formed on opposite
sides of the wrought iron ranch gates: on the right, "God,"
and on the left, "Muhammad." Athman got out of the car,
punched in the entry code, and the gate slowly opened. The
entrance drive was at least two hundred yards long and
slowly rose to open up onto extensive grounds. At the end

you could see the house, the typical all-white, American house with a large porch and columns. Athman, who apparently knew the place well, went around the house and parked in a kind of parking lot where there were about thirty cars. He then went to take his place under a large tent pitched for the occasion facing eastward to serve as a mosque. Once inside, Athman pointed out to me both Jamal and the owner of the property who were sitting next to the imam in the *mihrab*.

We were about thirty families in all. The women and children were in the house, pubescent boys were with the men in the tent.

Apparently we were the last to arrive. After prayers, the young Yemenite imam began his sermon from the pulpit:

"O Faithful Ones, men and women alike, may a community which acts for the best come forth from you, a community which commands *halal* and forbids *haram*, for it will be those that will succeed.

'TA-HA, We have not brought the Koran down to you in order to bring you unhappiness.' (S20, V1–2)

"*Ta-ha*, these are only two letters, and the heathens think that they constitute the first name given by God to his Prophet. A first name composed of two letters is less than a diminutive and for them it was proof that God has no respect for his Prophet. But, if we refer to the Arabic language in its basic form, *ta-ha* means 'you, the man, you, the human.' God addressed his Prophet: 'Ta-ha (O you who are human), we didn't have the Koran brought down to you to make you weary.'

"Made unhappy from its teachings, worn weary from its limits, and overworked from its interdictions? No! God specified:

'WE revealed the Book to you in full truth so that you may judge among people what God has shown you. But, do not become a defender of traitors.' (S4, V105)

"And also, so that you might unite your people and build a Nation, and open whole continents to the way of God, we brought down the Koran to you so that it may be applied according to the letter, word for word, vowel for vowel. We have given you this Book so it may become the reality of your Here and Now before becoming the reality of your Here-after. For the happiness, the greatness, and the honor of our Nation are the result of our return to the Koran, to reading and rereading it, to reflecting on it, to understanding it, and to applying it as the best medicine against all ills. Physical, moral, and political health are all in God's prescription: the Koran!

"This Book teaches us that one of the first questions asked of man is that of his destiny. What is his destiny? And for what is he predestined?

"Each man must answer these questions, whatever his culture, faith, belief. And if the majority of humanity has gone astray, it's because the best answers are in our Book. For us Muslims it's enough to join our destiny to Islam's in order to know for what we are intended, and the Koran will answer for us, to us, and about us. To us about ourselves, and to us in relation to others who are not of us or like us.

"This is why from the beginning of Islam the target of
the *Jahilites* has been the question of destiny and predesti-
nation. For them, if everything is fixed in writing and
decreed in advance by God, then how can man be held responsible for his acts? For them, to be overwhelmed by our
sins is unjust and if God knows everything about us, why
does He let us commit sins only to punish us afterward? It's
all ridiculous! Since it is written in the Koran:

'ALLAH leads astray those He wishes and leads back
to the straight path those He wishes.' (S35, V8)

'YOU can desire only if Allah desires.' (S76, V30)

"What the *Jahilites* didn't understand was that the will
of God, His power, His omniscience, His grandeur, and His
generosity as revealed in the Koran in no way negate man's
freedom to choose between obeying or disobeying, because
this 'free choice' accorded to man is in itself the will of God.
Therefore, the more powerful God's will, the greater is our
freedom to choose.

"As a result, when God proposed the freedom to
choose between obedience and disobedience to the elements of nature, they refused out of fear and asked God
to place them under His power for eternity, similar to the
men and the *jinn* who freely accept what God called 'a divine trust,' which is nothing other than free will. One might
be inclined to believe that God compels man to choose freedom. Not so! God, in His justice, does not force humans
to choose free will. Not so! Free will was offered by God
to humans and they accepted it.

'WE offered Our trust to the heavens, the earth,
and the mountains, but they refused to assume it
and were frightened by it. But man accepted it.'
(S33, V72)

"Another question must be asked: did the human being
give himself the freedom to accept? Or was it imposed by
God? It's clear that man is incapable of giving himself this
freedom without Allah's permission, so each aspect of existence depends on the will of the Creator. Those who venerate Him as well as those who disobey Him do so according
to His will. If man accepts God's proposal it's because he
understands its meaning, that is to say that it is the proof of
God's love for him, so that in the end he can say: 'Lord, we
love and obey You in total freedom, our submission is voluntary. We submit, but are not forced.'

"God wishes to be loved by free men, and the best way
for God to demonstrate His love for man is to award him
this freedom which is the foundation of his voluntary
submission.

"This is the meaning of free choice in Islam. God makes
you free so that you can choose to obey, and if you choose
to disobey, you are never free, because at that moment God
takes your freedom away from you because it is in His hands.
If God had decided to create humans in submission without the possibility of choosing, He would have done so.

"'IF We want, We can send down upon them from
the heavens a sign before which their necks will
be ever bowed in total submission.' (S26, V4)

"Besides, God in His generosity gave to man all the necessary elements of life (sun, water, air, all manner of plants, day, night . . .) so that man would be in His service. To this end God put all of nature at man's disposal so that he would not have to worry about existence. He need not be concerned with the order of things. God liberated man from the constraints of life. He relieved him of all such preoccupations in order to free him fully from excessive worries so that he might devote himself entirely to his faith and to his Creator.

"This is all part of a subtle and refined code made up of a collection of 'clear signs' so that man might know at every moment and in every circumstance that there is only one All-Powerful God who rules over everything. And to ensure that man recognizes these signs, God equipped him at birth with the tools of the senses: ears to hear, eyes to see, a tongue for speech, a brain for intelligence, understanding, analyzing, etc.

> 'GOD brought you out of your mothers' wombs in ignorance. He gave you hearing, sight, and intelligence so that you may give thanks.' (S16, V78)

"And if God wished these signs to be clear and unmistakable, explained the Sheikh Muhammad al-Shaarawi, 'it was so that man need not exhaust his intelligence looking for them. Man would see them, hear them, and feel them immediately. By clarifying these signs, God made our task easier so that we need not dwell on the process of creation to the point of forgetting about the Creator.'

"What's important is not how the universe is, or how it came into being, but who made it, why He made it, and for whom He made it.

"Thus, God gave us freedom of choice. But is this freedom absolute? No, no, and no! My brothers, it is made up of limits which are the privileged places of divine expression. Man cannot control his death because he does not control his birth, his dreams, or his sleep. Birth, death, and dreams are the exclusive domain of God where man can do nothing. God is great! God is great! God is great!

"The human being cannot choose his birth:

'IT is He who designs and fashions you in the wombs of your mothers as He wishes.' (S3, V6)

"Similarly, man cannot choose the time of his death:

'EACH nation has its end point. When it is reached, it cannot be prevented or delayed, not even for an hour.' (S7, V34)

"It is in the context of this freedom of choice that God has given us, that He will judge our ability to accept the limits He has set for us. To this end He puts us to the test in the life that we lead Here and Now so that He can make the final choice for us in our Hereafter: paradise or hell.

"Before I begin the chapter about life Here and Now and Hereafter, I would like to consider for a moment the question of parable and its truth in the Koran. It is said:

'O HUMANS! Here is a parable. Listen to it. Those that you call upon outside of God will never be able to create a fly, even if they all devote themselves to the task, and if a fly takes something away from them, they will not be able to retrieve it. How equal in weakness are both the searcher and what is sought.' (S22, V73)

"Fourteen centuries after this parable was transmitted by God to His Prophet, scientists teach us that as soon as a fly touches food, its decomposition begins so as to stimulate the insect's digestion.

"Their engineers, researchers, and experts who design planes, cars, and satellites could not restore the sugar cube to what it was before it was touched by the fly.

"O Believers! Listen and acknowledge the divine! The Koran is not afraid of science.

"The only parable used by God in the Koran, which seemed ordinary and stupid to the *kufar* because it referred to a fly, is confirmed and acknowledged by science. With the all-seeing knowledge of God, this parable preceded scientific knowledge. And to those who dare to say that the Koran is not fully scientific, you must reply that all of science is contained in the Koran. Here is how God called upon his Prophet:

'CREATE a parable for them about life in the Here and Now.' (S18, V45)

"Many among you, many who claim to be Muslim, live and think only according to life Here and Now. They are concerned only with the comfortable armchair of the Here and Now. They devote all of their energy and wealth in pursuit of the pleasures of life Here and Now. The Prophet tells us: *'God prescribed our duties, do not neglect them! He set the limits, do not overstep them! He prohibits certain things; do not transgress! He remains silent concerning others out of mercy not oversight; do not seek them out!'*

"O Believers! Death will remove all of you from Here and Now but it is in the life of the Hereafter that you will have to account for your actions.

"The Prophet rightly said: *'I do not fear for you in poverty. I fear for you when life Here and Now smiles kindly upon you, monopolizes you just as it has monopolized you, that it leads you astray just as you have lost your way. I do not fear for you in poverty, not at all, but for your life Here and Now.'*

"And to clarify my point I'll tell you a Jewish story. Why Jewish? Because it cannot be confirmed or denied. But if it can help us to understand this more clearly, why not use it? To the extent that one can benefit from a fable that does not interfere with our principles, it does no harm in the eyes of Islam, even if it's Jewish.

"As the story goes, a certain Sidna Aïssa (Jesus) was walking along the shore of Lake Tiberias when he was accosted by a traveler who proposed walking with him. Jesus said, 'Would you mind going to find us something to eat while I pray? I'm hungry.'

"A first reaction might be: Sidna Aïssa prayed to God because he was only a Prophet and not God, as claimed by the Christians, those falsifiers. . . . After, in the name of the All-Merciful God, it is said in the Sacred Book:

'SAY: God is He, the Unique.
God. The Supreme refuge.
He begot none nor was He begotten.
None could be His equal or like.' (S112)

"When the traveler came back with three chickens,
Sidna Aïssa was still praying. Out of impatience, the traveler ate one of the chickens. Sidna Aïssa finished his
prayers and asked the traveler what happened to the third
chicken. He replied: 'There were only two, O Prophet of
God.'

"Sidna Aïssa took a lamb that passed by, slit its throat,
skinned it and grilled it, then he asked God to resuscitate it.
And God resuscitated the lamb.

"O Believers! I point out to you that Sidna Aïssa asked
God to resuscitate the lamb, because only God can give back
life after death, because only God can perform miracles, and
Sidna Aïssa is only His Prophet.

"Sidna Aïssa said to the traveler: 'Be a witness to this
miracle and tell me where the third chicken went.' The traveler answered, 'O Prophet, there were only two.'

"Sidna Aïssa forced him over to the lake and made him
walk on the water with the help of God. Sidna Aïssa said
to him: 'Be a witness to this miracle and tell me where the
third chicken went.' The travler answered, 'O Prophet,
there were only two.' Sidna Aïssa sat down next to the
shore, made three piles of sand, and asked God to transform them into gold under the astonished eyes of the traveler. Sidna Aïssa then said to him: 'Be a witness to this
miracle!'

'O Prophet, I am a witness,' answered the traveler.

'This pile is yours, the second is mine, and the third goes to the one who ate the third chicken.'

'O Prophet! I am the one who ate the third chicken,' cried out the traveler.

"There it is, dear Believers, for the possessions of Here and Now, the traveler admitted the truth to the Prophet. Sidna Aïssa then said to him: 'All three are for you.' And he left him behind.

"Three mercenaries then come by and our despicable traveler finds himself in the middle of an American action movie. One of the mercenaries kills him. The first mercenary is then killed by the second who is killed by the third. This last one, while in the process of loading the gold onto his horse, ends up getting killed by the first mercenary in his last spurt of life.

"And so end the stories from the Here and Now. Four are dead and the gold given to the Prophet Aïssa by the miracle of God never goes anywhere.

"That's the way things end up in life in the Here and Now. The Prophets bring us wisdom, and the evil ones will always prefer gold. Which means that the world Here and Now will always remain in the state it's in now, but that each of us will leave in our own time for the Hereafter and the final judgment. God tells us:

'WHOSOEVER seeks a reward in this lowly world, let him be! God dispenses rewards of this world and the other. God hears and sees all.' (S4, V134)

"O Allah! I ask You to give me the strength to tell the truth in both peace and anger. I ask You to grant me the respect of moderation in the face of riches and in the face of poverty.

"May peace be with you."

At the end of the sermon, everyone got up to wish each other a happy feast while exchanging kisses and asking each other for forgiveness. Then we all headed over to the stables. The horse stalls were built in a circle which lined a large central courtyard of about fifteen yards in diameter with a recessed septic drain in the very center. The slaughter was set up in the middle of the courtyard. Three professional butchers, assisted by our host's servants, went about their business with the skill and deftness of magicians. Each of us went to pick out his sheep in one of the two stalls set aside for the animals about to be slaughtered.

The children, let loose by the women, filled the area of the sacrifice. Each adult surrounded by his male children would offer up the animal to the slaughterer, giving him the names of his mother, father, and children. This was the dedication of the sacrifice. Then, when the throats of the twenty-eight sheep were slit, the slaughterers began the work of skinning the animals. The first of the livers still warm and enveloped in their caul went directly to the already blazing fire-pits. This released odors which plunged me back to my childhood and brought tears to my eyes. To hide my sudden emotion, I went behind the fire-pits. My head lost in clouds of smoke, I cried, and my tears were camouflaged by the smoke. Perhaps I was a genuine Ishmael in the group and no one knew it, not even the servant who tried to get me to move away from the fire.

Outside, two long tables were set up covered with richly decorated white tablecloths upon which was displayed a buffet of grilled foods along with salads, rice, and all kinds of sauces. The feast began with God's blessing. A sound system played the best Koran recitations throughout the entire meal.

I asked Athman how he knew all these people.

"One day when I was in Silicon Valley, I made a presentation to the partners of the company on a new piece of software I had just developed. At the end of the meeting during the coffee break, Jamal came up to me to congratulate me and we struck up a conversation. He said to me, 'Congratulations. You've done good work. Personally, I didn't understand much of it, but my advisors convinced me of your effectiveness.' A bit surprised, I asked him, 'But . . . but have we met?' Then he answered, 'My name is Jamal Merouane and I'm the major shareholder of the company. I have some other investment projects I'd like to discuss with you.' I told him I was at his disposal, and that same evening we had dinner together at the house of some of his friends; Jamal never eats in restaurants. That was the night I left Silicon Valley to help set up the company where we work, which is totally owned by Jamal."

A bit stunned by what Athman just told me, I asked him, "So he's our boss?"

"He's your big boss."

"Life is pretty crazy. . . ."

"Life isn't crazy. God brings us all together with a little help from chance. We were destined to meet, Jamal, you, and I. We have a common destiny in the future. We were solitary streams, but we'll soon be the river."

At dessert they stopped playing the Koran recitations and young men were invited to recite poems on a small podium set up for the purpose next to the buffet. A young teacher from the Hamza mosque acted as master of ceremonies. He began with a thank-you speech: "My emirs, fathers, friends, on behalf of all those present, I would like to thank our host for having brought us together on this day of sacrifice so that we become a unified *Ummah* joined beyond exile and separation. He has brought us together and has united us in prayer, in celebration, and in mercy. May God bless him and increase his wealth, may He give him peace and serenity, O God ever-merciful!

"The first young poet you're going to hear is Foudid El Ali. He's a student in oral surgery. May God bless the poet's mouth and may God bless also his skill at healing unwell mouths; it's with great admiration that I give him the podium."

A young twenty-four-year-old with a Saudi-type goatee and black plastic American-type round glasses came up. He wore an Egyptian caftan, tight in the chest and shoulders but which billowed out from the waist and elbows making his gestures more dramatic and giving him the look of a noble peasant, his feet solidly planted on the ground ready to weather any storm. He adjusted the microphone, discreetly cleared his throat, and intoned:

I made my heart into a boat
And I embarked borne away by my pain
I left behind the peace of my soul
I tore up the sails of the vile and vain
Alone and fleeing, I face the sea.

The waves of injustice without recourse
Alone facing dawn, I sketch my loves
I kindle night's silence with my voice
I sing of the divine light before their laws
Alone and fleeing, I face night.

Stars, the guide to our paths
Dawn, the certitude of morning
God commands nature for us
How can we accept a mistake in the Writing?
Alone and fleeing, I face God.

The sermons in the mosques of the Greatest
Praise the dwarves who govern us
How can one not pray for a warrior's spirit?
What? Accept that they corrupt prayer?
Alone and fleeing, I face paradise.

If Muslims are truly rich,
Their paradise would be made up of *houris*
But the faithful have made a faith out of corruption,
To make their life hell is the only solution.
Alone and fleeing, I am my own solution.

The young poet left the podium amid warm and
sustained applause. The master of ceremonies accom-

panied him off and came back with the second poet he introduced:

"His name is Ahmed El Ghoufrani and he is a student in nuclear physics. He is skilled at putting together style, meter, and theme to bring forth the light of his words. If I weren't so sure of his faith, I would have said that the devil is trying to compete with the word of God."

The audience burst out laughing and the young poet went up to the microphone with such charisma that a respectful silence fell like magic, and he said, "This first poem is entitled 'I Hear Only God.'

> They will come crawling from the East
> And invading from the West
> It will be war.
> No! Do not say the traitor's name
> God will say it.
> Say! "I hear only God
> By faith in my land."

> They will come from heaven
> To defile Gabriel's space
> It will be war.
> No! Do not believe that they chose.
> God alone chose.
> Say! "I hear only God
> Even in the midst of thunder."

> They will come as always
> Testing their planes, their *babours*
> It will be war.

No! Do not say: "It's destiny"
Only God is master in this matter
Say! "I hear only God
Even in the middle of the sea."

High performance planes
And soldiers highly trained
It will be war.
No! Do not say: "They are mighty"
It is God who is Almighty
Say! I hear only God
Above and beyond their din."

So much money cast in the eyes of hunger,
To make wars with no tomorrow
That is war.
No! Do not say: "It was necessary"
Only a war for God is worthy.
Say! "I hear only God
I am a soldier in His war."

After applause, he continued calmly, "The second poem
is entitled 'The Great Ones of This World.'"

Great of this world
You who are perched on your thrones
From the depths of my tomb
I will be more elevated than you.
My mother gave birth to me as a Martyr
Death is my only desire.

Kill me! For my life is to be in death.
My death is in my life and my life in my death

The annihilation of my being is for me a gift from heaven
Keeping me alive is a mortal sin.
God's welcome is my only hope
To be born again in Him is my finest birth

I will approach His truth without a tremor
Say that I was born a Martyr.

My heart seethes with impatience
Injustices have tipped the scale
Should we continue to be silent
Or should we choose the beneficial sacrifice?

Say that I was born a Martyr
And death is my only desire.

At the end of the poem, the audience gave him a stand-ing ovation and clapped in rhythm to *Allahu Akbar* (God is great). The master of ceremonies, very moved, stammered, "God is great, my faithful brothers! God is great! On this great day of sacrifice we pledged to open your hearts to the true word, even if all present today are already convinced that truth is in the word of God. We thank you for your attention, and now, if you please, we'll meet in the tent for the afternoon prayers. For those among you who want to redo your ablutions, the courtyard where the sacrifices took place is now clean and available."

After the prayers, four- to five-pound packages of the sacrificial meat were put on the table in place of the buffet. Each of us took our portion for the *baraka*.

I took two packages, one for me and the other for my

mother. The rest of the meat would be given to the Hamza mosque to be distributed to the needy. Before taking leave of our host, we were expected to settle the price of our portion of the sheep with the bookkeeper. According to religious law, one sacrifices only what one can pay for. The minimum price of the animal was set, but anyone could give more according to his means, the money would also be sent to the Hamza mosque.

It must have been 4 p.m. when we left the ranch. Athman dropped me off at my place and said, "Bye, and kiss your dog good night."

Back at the apartment, a sinister silence echoed after I opened the door and closed it behind me. Jenny was on the bed finishing her novel. Keytal was shut out on the balcony, and didn't even deign to greet me by pawing at the window. On this feast of *Eid* when humanity put aside violence in favor of sacrifice, I had the feeling that I was about to be offered up as a sacrifice for having ruined Keytal and Jenny's day. Jenny, usually very sweet and easygoing, let her anger take over. She greeted me with, "Oh, it's you," which made me feel like I had just dropped in out of nowhere.

"So did it go well?" she added.

"Yes . . ."

"Yes, what?"

"Yes, it was great."

"Was everything done properly?"

"What do you mean?"

"Without woman, dog, wine, with sheep, with prayer . . . everything that makes God happy and human beings sad."

"You're a believer, aren't you?"

"Yes, but not in the same things."

"All faith is irrational because it's transcendent."

"In that case, crazy people can become transcendent."

"There are a lot of idiots who also have a transcendental stupidity. Now enough of this game . . . because God is going to bear the brunt of it. For me, it's much simpler. Right now I'm having a problem with religion, or rather, religion is becoming the answer. So when I commit, I follow it, and when I believe, I act."

"Who's stopping you from acting?"

"No one is, but according to Islam, Keytal can't live with us anymore."

"You want me to get rid of my dog because you're rediscovering God?"

"No! I'll go find a studio apartment nearby where you can come to see me."

"What are you talking about? We're going to separate because of a dog? Isn't the dog one of God's creatures?"

"Yes, and the pig is also one of God's creatures, but we don't eat it."

"But I'm not asking you to eat Keytal!"

"And I'm telling you I can't live with him anymore."

"Before, when you didn't believe in anything, you acted like you had faith and now that you're becoming a believer, you can't even stand a dog anymore?"

"I want to find myself and if you want to help me, fine, but if you want to give me a hard time, forget it!"

"I'm trying to understand."

"There's nothing to understand. My destiny calls for it and I have to live it out. I want to live it out."

"But we have a past and you have a past with Keytal.
Can't your faith include these pasts?"

"I'm having enough trouble with my own past . . . so
to think about the one I have with a dog . . ."

Jenny went out on the balcony. Despite light clothing and a chill in the air, she sat down on the floor and
cradled Keytal in her arms. Through the window I saw her
back slumped in sadness and her white arms intertwined
with the dog's paws. The dog rested his head on her shoulder and gave me a distraught look. It's true he wasn't used
to this kind of thing. Jenny tried to calm herself down by
calming the dog, who was probably wondering what was
going on with me.

I understood that all this was very upsetting for her.
She had set everything up right down to the finest detail so
that we would be like in the *Song of Songs*:

> *Longing for him in love,*
> *I sat down*
> *in the shadow of the one*
> *I had so desired.*

For her, the *Song of Songs* is a fountainhead, the water
which irrigates the earth so that it may flower. In her mind,
love is cultivation. You have to cultivate poetry to be
grounded in love. For Jenny, talking about everyday life already defiles our emotions. "Give me a glass," "pass me the
bread," "what should we eat?" "where did you put the keys?"
are statements that are just as polluted as polluting. Jenny
mythifies silence as a meaningful yet unarticulated language.

It's an albino language without phonemes, listened to hyper-
sensitively, in the depth of sighs and in the burst of emotions.
Her faith is love, her perfection is work, and her religion is
building. She is a walking temple, and each one of her gestures is a wordless sermon, an act of faith.

An architect by profession, Jenny defended her doc-
toral thesis on "The Sacred in the Construction of Habi-
tat: Materials, Forms, Structures, and Orientations." She
subscribes to the kind of construction that brings the forms
of nature together. For her the sacred is about embracing
nature because it's God's creation, and what could be more
sacred than nature just as God made it? Architecture which destroys natural sites in order to impose regular, abstract forms is desecration. That's why a large pos-
ter of Frank Lloyd Wright's *Fallingwater* hung above our
bed.

Jenny is an only child, the daughter of doctors. The
apartment we live in is her mother's former office. After her
parents moved to their country house, her mother preferred
to have her office there too. All that, as Jenny says, "so that
she and I might get to know each other better and construct
our life as a couple on solid ground and not in the clouds."
The apartment had been given to us as a laboratory for our
love.

Being brought up as only children drew us closer together, and sometimes I saw Jenny more as a sister than a
lover. This idea was jarring to her sense of puritanism, and
so she preferred to talk about friendship between us rather
than as being brother and sister, which would have been in-
cestuous. She used to recite:

Ah! If you were my brother
If you had been nursed by my mother
I would kiss you when we meet in the street
I would do so without shame
I would have you enter my mother's house
I would be your guide
And you, my master
I would anoint you
With the perfumed liquor
Of tears
Of my pomegranate
With your left hand under my head
Embrace me with your right.

I took out a DVD of one of Bilal's sermons, and began to listen to it. Bilal is a black imam of Ethiopian descent. Bilal has an exceptional charm. He is so gifted at crafting American English into beautiful forms that after a few minutes it was like hearing Arabic. As soon as Jenny heard the religious chants that come before the sermon, she left Keytal and came straight up to me, furious, placing herself between the screen and me.

"You mean black imams aren't 'satans' in Islam?"

"Quit joking around. Islam is the only religion which isn't racist."

"Maybe not when it comes to men, but certainly it is for dogs."

"Have it your way."

"Anyway, I'm leaving you with your Bilal. I'm going out with my Keytal."

"Please don't mix these things up."

"I still haven't figured out what things you're getting mixed up with."

Jenny locked herself in the bathroom and came out a bit later red-eyed and in jogging clothes. Keytal waited for her quietly at the door. She attached his leash and dragged him outside slamming the door behind her.

Finally I was alone with Bilal.

"O Believers, it's true that the Muslim world is going through several crises. The rich are living in moral poverty, a crisis in faith, and the believers are living in material poverty which constantly tests their faith. How can we put the rich on the right track so that they will sustain the poor? And so that some kind of balance of resources be established at least within the Muslim community?

"If the rich man is rich, it's because God is putting his generosity to the test, and if the poor man is poor, it's God's way of putting his patience to the test. The rich man's generosity is what God wills in order to relieve the poor man of his woes. If the rich man becomes greedy, poverty would no longer be just a simple putting to the test; it would become a permanent state, something which goes against God because God never wanted his people to be poor and miserable.

"God divided earthly goods in a seemingly unjust way between the exceedingly rich and the exceedingly poor. Why is that? Solely to offer an opportunity, a possibility, a clear choice to man to do right by his faith.

'CALL to the faith and follow the straight path as
you have received the order to do so; respond not
to their passions and proclaim: I believe in the
Books God has revealed; I have received the order
to judge among you equitably and in all justice.
God is our Lord and theirs.' (S42, V15)

"God shuffles the deck. By mixing the kings with the
jacks, he teaches the kings to see themselves through their
jacks, and the jacks to see themselves as kings in the eyes of
God. God created order within nature. This order will never
change. It is fixed until the last judgment. But Satan sows
seeds of disorder in the human heart. Humans must learn
how to restore order within themselves and within their
emotional and material lives in the Here and Now.

'O CHILDREN of Adam! Let not the devil tempt
you, as he did your parents. He caused them to
go out of Paradise undressing them to expose
their genitals.' (S7, V27)

"God points out, designates, illuminates. His teaching
is illumination, but life surrounding us is darkness. That is
why the absolute duty of each human is to continually seek
out God's way among thousands of paths and not to be led
astray down the wrong paths.

'AND if the devil provokes you into doing evil,
seek refuge beside God. For He hears and knows
all.' (S7, V200)

"Abu Talib al Makki in his work *Nourishment of Hearts* said: 'Know that most sins committed by humans are caused by two things: lack of patience at times of tribulation and a lack of control over their emotions.'

"And God tells us:

'WE have truly created man so that he may endure hardship.' (S90, V4)

"By speaking thus, is God being unkind to us? No! Does God wish us to suffer? No! Does God wish to mistreat us? No! Does He wish to inflict harm on us? No! So what does God want? God wishes us to endure misery, poverty, envy, luxury, and wealth. God wishes to teach us how to earn paradise. God wishes to instruct us how to love Him, which can only be done by learning how to love the world, the universe, the stars, life, and death. Learning how to love God means learning how to endure, to love, to live and to die. Those who do not struggle against their passions do not love God. Those who fear death do not love God.

"Faithful Brothers, when you love God and devote yourselves to God, you are not doing a service to God, but to yourself. Believing in God does not help God to become more powerful, it helps you to become stronger because God is just, He is justice itself. But God does not punish every fault, He does not prosecute every infraction. God gave Guidance, He charted the path for us, and it will be the way we follow this path that will determine our judgment on the day we all gather before God.

'SAY: Our Lord will bring us together, and He will judge between us equitably. He is the supreme judge.' (S34, V26)

"Thus dear Faithful Ones, God is Judge and All-Knowing. By virtue of being All-Knowing, He is the most just in His judgment. What do the police do when they conduct an investigation? They want to find out what the criminal is hiding, and as a result of this knowledge they expose the guilty parties in an attempt to render justice. Nothing can be hidden from God. He knows all, He is All-Knowing.

"God does not need investigators to search for clues, fingerprints, motives to know who sinned and who didn't. It's because God knows everything that He is the best of judges, the Judge of judges.

"In the sacred Book, God teaches us how to render justice among us, how to punish thieves, swindlers, adulterers, and those who steal from orphans. All of that was dictated to us by God and He will judge us according to the way we administer this justice. In each courtroom in this lowly world of ours, God is present, regardless of the religion of the victim or of the judges, because there is no justice in this lowly world without His justice, there is no just punishment without the fear of the ultimate punishment, there is no equity unless it is weighed on the scale of God.

'O YOU believers! Watch over God's law with rectitude and witness in all fairness, let not the hatred of a people prevent you from committing an injustice. Be just: Justice is very close to piety. Fear God, because He knows all your actions.' (S5, V8)

"God created us weak, mortal, and impotent. This is not to secure His power; He is powerful! But to require us to rise above our own weakness, mortality, powerlessness, and the power of God and His true place is to be found in this rising up. That is where you should place your faith. God said to His Prophet:

'FOLLOW what is revealed to you and wait patiently until God pronounces His judgment. He is the best of judges.' (S10, V109)

"O Believers! Look how clear the message from God is. He said to His Prophet:
'Say': in other words speak, speak forth your word.
'Follow what is revealed to you:' God gives him the direction for his action.
'Until the time of God's judgment:' God defines for him the limits of his free choice.
'Be patient:' God asks him to wait, He reassures him by telling him that He is the best of judges. That is true! God is the best of judges. This clarity exists so that we might readily understand God's demands, and thus quickly apply them and become loved by God.
'O Allah! To You I submit myself, in You I believe, from You I ask assistance, to You I return, through You I struggle, from You

I accept judgment. Forgive what I have done, what I have hidden and what I have revealed. It is certainly You who speed up and slow down time, no divinity other than You.'

"May peace be with you."

Even though I had listened to these words dozens of times, I continued to be struck by the clarity of language which joined the simple to the essential. A language which divides the world up simply in order to make a simple place for us and to define a simple role for us. I then understood how millions of people could accept to live according to such a naïve conception rather than having to confront the modern world in its complexity. At the same time as Bilal's voice is supportive and humane, it is harsh and authoritarian. And if at times it is doctrinaire, it's because he is speaking to overwhelmed believers. Each time I hear this voice it makes me feel swept up in a dance of whirling dervishes while being held in the arms of my absent father.

Laws designed for human jurisdiction are made in the image of man: small and narrow with interpretations limited to concerns of justice applied in a uniform fashion out of concern for equality. The laws of God are far reaching so as to give God precedence over men. Judgments and condemnations are passed under His watchful eye. At this point the law is not as important as the way it is applied, which serves as a testimony of one's love or scorn of God, for He is always there to judge those who judge. A world without the judgment of judges is no longer divine, and a world that loses its sense of the divine has nothing sacred left within it. When judges make and enforce the laws, their

justice is by extension ethically inferior to the justice designed by religion, because the judges of the latter are
watched over by the Highest Judge. At the basis of secular
justice rests the contradiction of men seeking to extend their
reach beyond their own human weakness. It was this idea
of a judge above all others that convinced me to buy my first
Koran.

The next day I brought my mother her portion of the *Eid*
lamb and accompanied her to the cemetery to visit my father. She was wearing the Chanel suit that my father had
given her for their twentieth wedding anniversary and all
of her finest jewelry covered by her raincoat buttoned up
to her neck.

"You know how I am, my son," she said, "I don't go to
the celebration of feasts, but I do like to dress up like this in
the spoils of our exile when I go to visit your father. I'm sure
that it pleases him."

As we were heading out the door, she noticed that she
didn't have her car keys: "I don't know where I put them!"

She ran back to her bedroom.

My mother had stopped working in laboratory research to become a consultant for a large company specializing in genetically modified plants. She enjoyed great respect
from her colleagues and fellow workers for all that she had
done, even though this unanimous opinion was never expressed publicly. My mother was the most famous of anonymous scientists. Just to tease her I used to say that she was
so afraid of losing her roots due to genes destroyed from
exile that she ended up specializing in genetic manipulation.

I never really understood what connections she drew between her faith and science. And when I started to study science in middle school, I used to ask her very specific questions about her work. She would always answer in a reassuring tone: "I improve plants. I do not invent new animal species."

When she was younger, she had a way of rolling her r's with an emphasis that gave away her feelings. As she got older, she softened her r's, making them sound less forceful but deeper. My mother had a real talent for making herself seem insignificant, even transparent. It wasn't in her to call attention to herself. Her main purpose in life was to do, and she learned to do what no one else could do as well. She made corn and wheat resistant to all manner of insects, and she multiplied their yield. If she invented things that made the world take notice, it was simply because her mind only worked in that direction. Only she knew how to make herself resistant to the effects of exile, life's adversity, and mental corrosion. It seemed as if my mother knew how to talk to her own genes and modify her hormonal balance, secreting chemical substances that made her impervious to all influences at any moment. This made her seem to exist outside of time, as if she wondered whether she was still human. She was so genetically modified that she herself no longer knew the original stock she came from. Was she corn, wheat, fruit or vegetable? The one distinctive gesture that she saved for me was the way that she caressed my face, a caress that was embedded in the deepest layer of her past, her culture, and her origins. Perhaps, in the end, she had changed everything within her in order to safe-guard this gesture as the only physical and ancestral inherit-ance that she could pass on to me.

The more my own faith strengthened, the more I thought that my mother had sublimated all that she was. It was hard to see her as a great scientist, given the way she had managed to become on the inside what no one from the outside could imagine, and to be totally different on the outside from what she was on the inside. In a different way, she was complete in each of her two worlds. Because she lived them as contra-dictory, she kept them so separate. She could move out of being a Lebanese woman to passing for an Irish American in an effortless physical movement without the slightest misstep or confusion. Yet, with her artist's sensitivity, she went be-yond her sublimated self to give me this special gesture.

"There, I found the keys! They were in a jacket pocket in the closet."

She handed me the keys and we took the elevator down to the parking garage. On our way, we stopped at the flo-rist shop where my mother would order a rose each time she went to visit my father. She gave the exact change to the florist who then gave her the rose and wished her a good afternoon.

We set off for the cemetery in silence. It was part of a ritual that had taken shape over time in response to my mother's moods. Out of total despair, and to keep my fa-ther close to us, she had decided to bury him here, even if it went against the wishes of his family, who wanted his body returned home to Egypt.

Each time we made this trip, I felt that she was still uncertain of that decision.

When we arrived near the grave site, I parked the car in the same spot as always. We reached the grave in almost the same number of steps. She unbuttoned her raincoat to expose her jewelry and then wiped off the surface of his photo attached to the tombstone. The photograph depicted him playing golf in a precise movement hitting a ball with the club raised above his head in perfect alignment, a pose that exhibited the elegance and strength of his body. And since the photo is affixed to a slab of marble vertical to the tombstone, it appears as if he is trying to thrust his own remains off into the distance beyond the tomb.

With hands open to the heavens, we read the *Fatiha,* the opening sura of the Koran. Then my mother placed the rose on the grave and we left.

On one of our visits, not paying attention, I had placed the rose on the tomb before the prayer and my mother had had me remove it immediately.

"If you put the rose down before you pray, it's as if you're praying to the rose instead of to your father. So first the prayer, then the rose."

My mother's symbolic imagination could not live without scientific rigor. But in the end, her insistence on such precise gestures in relation to these visits was designed to circumscribe her own pain and help her get used to what she knew she would never get used to. Repeating these gestures was an attempt on her part to ritualize her suffering, to caress the wound and soothe the torture that it produced. The death of my father had made my mother hard as tempered steel, at a time in her life when she was just starting to distance herself from the prospect of returning to her homeland. His death plunged her into a new kind of exile, unexpectedly brutal, which left her to face an unanticipated solitude. Reducing a family of three to two amounted to killing one third of it within each of us. My mother never said anything about her suffering. She had worked so hard not to become one of those uncompromising Arab and Mediterranean mothers with their explosive and castrating manner, that she had lost all sense of how to converse. Her speech was precise; her perfect choice of words and her silence never lacked eloquence. She would listen to women's chatter without participating, and when one of the aunts or cousins would call on her to join in, she would answer: "I'm listening." Often she would say: "In the face of injustice, words often make bad lawyers. It makes you wonder how justice can work."

II

During a coffee break at the office, I decided to take up this question of dogs in Islam with Athman, in the hope that this was just a phobia. Deep down, I wanted to hear that this was because of his own hatred of dogs and not due to Islam, but Athman reacted violently, shouting, "I have absolutely nothing against dogs!"

"But isn't there a way to manage this little 'indelicacy' considering how much I love this animal?"

Athman was horrified to hear how much love I had for Keytal. He couldn't fathom such feeling.

"Love? For a dog?"

"Yes, I do love Keytal!"

"Poor Raouf, all of the love you carry within you and all of the love you are capable of is only an infinitesimal portion of the love that you should have for God, your family, and your brothers. Meanwhile you give yourself the luxury of wasting it on a dog?"

"It's not the same kind of love."

"And to top it all off, you have a catalogue of different kinds of love."

"That's a bit much. . . ."

"Love is unique, one of a kind. It's like water in the middle of a desert: hard to find, yet you need a lot of it."

Athman's unyielding nature, regardless of the topic, was irritating. The rigidity of his argumentation was stifling, so I changed the subject: "Let's talk about something else."

"You're the one who keeps going over the wrong problems."

"It sounded weird to me, that's all. Before I make a final decision, I wanted to be sure."

"What decision is that?"

"To leave Jenny's and find myself a studio apartment."

"Nothing could be easier. After work, we'll go to Jamal's and you'll have your keys."

"Why? Does he own a rental company?"

"He owns every kind of thing, even if very little is actually in his name. He's like all big shots; everything is theirs but nothing is kept in their name."

Our office cafeteria was on the top floor of the building. It was in a circular form with one half lined with windows and an open roof. The coffee, beverage, and sandwich machines were built into the wall on one half of the room and were visually integrated into an abstract mural across the entire wall. In the seating area there were small bistro tables on one side where you could have a quick bite to eat, and large comfortable armchairs for relaxing on the other.

Before Athman, I used to come here for coffee and try to drift off. I had a lot of trouble disconnecting myself from my work and letting my imagination run free. The abstract painting provided an aesthetic substitute that did my dreaming for me. But since Athman, I felt I barely even recognized this place anymore. And even though the theological bent of our discussions was founded in abstraction, Athman's discussions would pull me out of this futuristic setting and define the real. The ultramodern look of this space would weigh me down while the archaic language of Athman's religious arguments would propel me upward. I was sure that God had put Athman in my life so that I could see myself differently and discover the person I really was. Athman uncovered my true identity, the one that I had always kept in check so I could finish my studies, not upset my parents, maintain a certain distance from the country of my roots, and question the country of my birth still in keeping with my parents' principles. Everything had been decided for me a priori to such an extent that even my nationality was a priori. Thankfully in the Hereafter of all of that, there is God. I felt born within me a brand new feeling toward Athman, like something I had never felt before toward a person I was close to. I greatly admired him. I had always had heroes, but only basketball players or movie stars. I liked one for the way he dribbled, the other for the way he brought a character to life, but my burgeoning admiration for Athman was tautological. It integrated being and thought.

Without realizing it, I ended this inner reflection with a deep sigh which made Athman react. "After a sigh like that, you must always ask forgiveness from God (*astaghfir Allah*), because that kind of deep sigh signals a thought gone astray, like yawning is the sign of being sleepy. That's what's fantastic about God: He directs, He regulates, He responds to everything right down to the slightest detail. It's magnificent that the greatness of God in Islam is not only the greatness of power; it is especially the greatness of presence. Islam is great because God is always present. He never lets anyone down."

I was struck by his silence. Usually when he got going on a major point about God, he wouldn't end so quickly. After a lull I felt obliged to say something.

"Now it seems like you're the one lost in thought."

"A little bit . . . Say, didn't you do some work at Boeing after you finished your degree?"

"Yes. I was there for a year."

"What did you do there?"

"I worked on the development of software for monitoring in-flight conditions. I was involved with what were called 'technical parameters,' that is, everything related to the plane itself. I didn't work on the external forces such as wind conditions, climate, etc. I concentrated on small private planes, not big ones."

"Do you still know people who work there?"

"I'd have to check. Why? Do you need something?"

"Jamal told me that he had placed an order for some software that would make navigation so simple that even an inexperienced pilot could fly."

"That's impossible! Exterior conditions are too unpredictable even in mid-flight. From the number of passengers to the total weight of the aircraft, everything affects the flying of the plane. In flight navigation, there are more variables than constants. A subway system without a conductor is easy to design, but not a plane without a pilot. And it won't be discovered anytime soon, either. Now, take the Israelis. They're champions at constructing small spy planes with no pilots. But once the plane accomplishes its mission, it self-destructs. Just about two years ago I think they managed to create a plane that could return to the base by itself, but it certainly had to be controlled from land."

"Please, when you have to give me an example, pick anyone you want, but not Jews. I get so pissed off and worked up that it makes my heart beat out of control. I feel like ripping things apart. Without realizing it, I get carried away."

"But you know that in a number of ways they really know what they're doing."

"Are you defending them?"

"No, I'm not defending anyone! I'm just objectively informing you."

"I will never be objective when it comes to Jews because objectivity weakens you. A real combatant needs to remain vigilant in his resolve to fight. And that *is* real subjectivity! I try to protect my subjectivity at all costs and to hell with objectivity."

As we waited for the elevator to take us to the laboratory, he winked at me to tell me to act as if nothing was going on. Then he started lecturing me in a loud voice so that everyone around us could hear: "You've got to stop smoking. Every time I drink my coffee in the smoking section of the café, I leave feeling dizzy. And if you don't, I'll have to tell your wife that you still haven't stopped smoking."

"I'll try. . . ."

Everyone near us looked ready to burst out laughing, but when they saw my sheepish look, they held back, as if they had missed something serious.

Once inside the laboratory, we burst out laughing and Athman said:

"Didn't I tell you they were just like big children?"

Then he called Jamal to set up a meeting. When he hung up, he said, "Tonight we'll have dinner with him."

"Already?"

"Yes. With him everything is always quick and easy."

"Where will we meet?"

"At his place, because Jamal never eats out. How many times do I have to tell you that?"

Athman decided that we should leave work a little earlier than usual so we could arrive at Jamal's in time to say the late afternoon prayers together.

"A communal prayer is always better," he said.

We passed through an upscale area and, facing a large park, Athman stopped and pointed to Jamal's building, a five-floored cylindrical structure with a larger diameter penthouse where Jamal lived. It consisted of three apartments: one for him, one for his wives, and one for his servants. The terrace was also his. It was a hanging garden landscaped with a rosemary hedge and miniature palms that withstood the cold but never bore fruit. Jamal commented, "A country where palm, fig, and olive trees can't produce fruit is not to be trusted."

Between Athman's nervousness and his fear of being late, we got there forty-five minutes early. He suggested that we walk around the park. For him, it was also a chance to debrief me about Jamal.

"Jamal broke with his 'dynasty' over the Gulf War. He did not accept that Kuwait refused to forgive any debt owed by Iraq. Whenever he brings this up, he'll say: "For a few million dollars, they went as far as a fratricidal war, and worst of all they let non-Muslims call the shots, the same *kufar* whose boots trampled on the sacred soil of the Kaaba. Of course, the Americans are our allies, but they're also unbelievers. It's still their fault. They have intelligence and strategy on their side. As for our side, history traps us like the trick question on an exam: name the countries of the twentieth century which were the richest on the planet and the most insignificant politically speaking. . . ."

At this hour, people were returning from work, taking their dogs out for a walk. When I saw all those poodles, boxers, and German shepherds jumping all over the place, I felt a pang. I missed Keytal terribly and I was sure that at this very moment, he couldn't possibly understand the distress he felt because of my absence. I thought that it was really unfortunate that in Islam dogs were considered only according to standards of hygiene. Scarcely had I begun to sort out my feelings when Athman said: "Look at all these dogs that crap everywhere! What a shitty society!"

I answered him back. "But there's nothing shitty about having a dog."

He acted as if he hadn't heard me and went on about Jamal.

"Jamal was born in a Florida clinic, grew up between London where he did all of his studies and Kuwait City where he spent his vacations. As a child, his trips to Kuwait were a return to his youth and to the company of women in the harems. During puberty, he went back to religious training, and once adolescence set in, he would sneak off to the seashore to a world of drugs and fast cars. Between two and five in the morning while the city slept, the rich sated and the poor exhausted, Jamal and his friends would just be coming back from their night on a yacht spent eating, drinking, smoking, and even snorting. Because on Kuwaiti soil, the rule of Islam forbade the sale of alcohol and meeting with women outside of places sanctioned by Islam. So to get around the law, they would take to the open sea. In the predawn hours, Jamal's yacht would dock not far from the main café to drop him and his friends off on the beach before heading back to the marina. They would pick up their cars and on the coastal corniche between the two curves and the main café, they would get their kicks betting on races where BMWs, Jaguars, Rolls-Royces, Ferraris, and Mustangs would perform breakneck stunts like bronco riders in a rodeo. Often they would break away just when one of the cars would veer off the road to end up against a lamp post or wall. They'd get home before the ambulances arrived. Those were their game rules, the rules and regulations of their craziness. It was their *Rebel Without a Cause*, gandura-style.

"Until the day when Jamal lost control of his Porsche and mowed down several yards of grass before ramming into

an abstract sculpture in a public park. Jamal walked away
unscathed, but the brother sitting next to him was hit by a
concrete block square in the head and died on the spot. The
shock was terrible for Jamal. The doctor of the emirate
advised psychoanalysis. After much research and many appointments, Jamal first decided to eliminate female doctors,
on the pretext that he couldn't tell them everything unless
they slept with him, and even then. . . . As for men, he put
them in two categories: those in their forties whom he dis-
missed because for him they all looked like homosexuals; and
those between fifty and sixty, the only ones he considered
to be serious. Among these, he picked the most famous, the
most expensive, and the least decrepit.

   "From his very first session, Jamal felt uncomfortable.
He would repeat over and over: 'I'm the one who pays and
instead of him telling me what's wrong, I'm supposed to tell
him what's wrong. What a rip-off!'

   "One of his cousins tried in vain to explain that the
process of psychoanalysis involved telling the psychoana-
lyst what you thought wasn't right inside of you, so that with
help of the shrink you could understand what was really
wrong with you, but not immediately apparent. To the idea
that the shrink's role is to help us understand what's wrong
and bring our feelings back in line with the reality that corresponds to them, Jamal would answer: 'But to get there, I
have to tell him everything about my family, my mother, my
father. First of all, that's not how we do things, and besides,
my parents' life is so complicated that I don't even know the
whole story myself. My father's harem has over forty women
and I have more than thirty brothers and sisters. With the

little that I know, I could never be cured. And in the final analysis, he'll tell me that the sins I commit are determined by the sins my parents made in raising me, and that in order to see my way out of it, I'd have to recognize the sins of my parents in order to come to grips with my own sins. But because I am not God, I can't forgive the sins of my parents, and besides, this is totally incompatible with Islam. Islam says that with faith you must manage your life in the Here and Now in order to earn life in the Hereafter, which means using faith to avoid the devil and never resorting to psychoanalysis, which neutralizes the devil and teaches you how to live with him. Healing at this cost amounts to selling your soul.'

"He refused to listen to his cousin's explanation that 'psychoanalysis is based on dreams,' and would reply: 'That's just it. We don't have the same conception of dreams. What these Judeo-Christians don't understand is that a true Muslim, a practicing believer, is entirely Muslim or not at all Muslim. In Islam, faith does not tolerate halfway measures, and in order to live in their world, a Muslim has to slalom like crazy to avoid the wrong paths. Everything is set up for them and against us. We can only profit fully from their society by losing a big part of ourselves. I would even go so far as to say that their society is set up so that we Muslims will lose our souls.'"

Then Athman looked at his watch and said: "We were early, but we'll end up being late."

At the end of our walk, we came to the elevator of the building. Once inside the elevator, I asked him: "So in the end did he go through with psychoanalysis?"

"Of course not! Not a chance!"

"So you mean we're going to see a sick man?"

"Don't be silly. He was healed by faith."

As we reached the floor of Jamal's apartment, one of his servants opened the door and showed us into a room, and handed each of us a djellaba, slippers, and a towel before pointing us toward the bathroom. Then he said, "Do your ablutions. Sidi will join you for prayer. He's not far away, so if you need something, just pick up the phone and I'll answer."

Athman, used to being here, took his shower, did his ablutions, and went into the living room. I did the same. Although he thought of himself as my spiritual guide, he was, in fact, only a guide in practical matters. Jamal arrived draped in white, smelling of musk, and holding a magnificent set of prayer beads made out of green stones of Eilat. In response to my gaze, he explained,

"These are anti-Israeli prayer beads. We keep track of our prayers on their stones, and we'll see to which of us this land reverts in the end."

After we finished the sunset prayers, we moved to the table. Jamal took the phone off the hook and left the receiver on the stacking tables. With a remote control he turned on a CD of a cappella religious chants, and commented on his musical selection:

"This kind of chant is relaxing and draws us close to God and it also interferes with wiretapping. . . . So then, what brings you here?"

Athman explained that I was looking for a studio apartment. Then he explained that I wanted to repent and that I would be honored if he would accept to become my spiritual guide and accompany me in this process. He added that I had all the qualities of a 'martyr of God.'"

Jamal listened carefully, then picked up a business card and a pen from the stacking tables. He wrote down the numbers 23/18 on the card, signed it, and gave it to Athman, saying, "Go to the Maïmouna agency and give this card to Faisal. He'll know what needs to be done."

Then he turned and asked me my name. I answered, and he again replied to Athman, "As for Raouf's confession, I'll talk to the imam of the Hamza mosque, the one who was there the day of the *Eid*, and we'll see what to do. But for now, *bon appétit* everyone."

What amazed me the most was how no sooner was a thing said than it was done. It seemed as if the solutions came before the problems, and that no one had to waste time thinking about the problems. That would have been time taken away from the practice of our faith. It was necessary to dispense with problems as quickly as possible, and not worry about those that couldn't be resolved, because it might distract us too much. And, yet, the irresolvable problems that presented themselves to Muslims were not insignificant.

While serving us appetizers, Jamal asked us if we knew about the two suicide bombings that took place that day in Palestine. Athman answered, "We vaguely heard about it on the radio on our way here."

"The courage of these young martyrs is magnificent," said Jamal.

Athman added, "The adults ought to be ashamed. These teenagers understand what fighting for Islam is all about while the adults just look on twiddling their thumbs."

Jamal was pleased when Athman picked up with, "Cowardice has its limits when honor is abused."

In this kind of discussion, Athman stopped eating and drinking. He put down his fork and raised his knife like the conductor of an orchestra and announced, "I truly admire these young martyrs. Nothing counts more for a Muslim than his relation to God. In times of peace, he lives his life in the Here and Now as God's trial for the last judgment. But in times of war, it's as if God puts him to the test by using death as a means of returning to Him. Because no Muslim would ever conceive of going to war for any reason except for God. For a Muslim, nothing in this lowly existence on earth justifies giving up life, not even country, truth, or justice. Only God deserves our death, because He is country, truth, and justice unto Himself, and also because He alone can give back life. This means that one never dies for God. The difference between an Israeli soldier and a Palestinian martyr is that the Israeli dies for the promise of God while the Palestinian dies for God. Which of the two is more ridiculous? Which one is consistent with his beliefs?"

Instinctively, I said, "But the soldier doesn't bring about his death."

"No one brings about his own death. It's God who decides for the soldier and the martyr."

Athman had lashed out at me with such anger that Jamal felt compelled to intervene and break the tension in the air. "In this life, you can die as a result of error, lust, or vice, but in each case, we are at the mercy of God's judgment, regardless of the death we suffer. If so, then you may as well die for Him. I'll tell you the story of how I came to repent, and may it serve as an example to Raouf who has also decided to repent.

"Three years ago, I was in a New York hotel room with two supposedly 'AIDS-free' prostitutes. I had been drinking and eating for three days straight without ever getting sober. When I turned on the TV I saw a documentary on Hawaiian tourism. Four days later, I woke up on one of these same beaches, in the company of the bellboy. He explained how this happened: while I was watching this show on TV, I called the bellboy, pointed to the TV and told him, 'I want to go to the beach on the screen with the two girls, and I designate you as the guide.' Then I gave him my credit card and PIN. The bellboy set up the trip and even brought his wife along. I was totally unconscious when I made the trip. To this day, I have no recollection whatsoever. All I know is that I was in a hotel room in New York and then I woke up on a beach in Hawaii. Between the two there was a total void of five days. When the imaginary and real worlds get confused in your head and you become a television set, it's no longer the devil manipulating you: you've become the devil. That was my last voyage into madness. Since then, I've stopped alcohol, drugs, and television, and if I have a television in the house, it's only to watch the news. I'm back on the straight path, and it's thanks to Islam that I've learned little by little to control my impulses, my bank account, my spending, and my life. I married a Libyan woman and I have three servants at home, all Comoran Muslims: four women under my roof, all permitted by God. My money works for me, and I work for the glory of God."

"It's really fantastic. To remain humble in your dependence on God with the means that you have. I think it's fantastic."

"The fortune is God's; I am only one of His humble servants."

Before leaving the table, Athman uttered a *dawah* of thanks. We took leave of Jamal, who accompanied us to the landing. Athman kissed him on the shoulders and on the tip of his nose according to the true Bedouin tradition. As for me, I shook his hand quickly and rushed into the elevator.

It must have been 11:30 as we drove through the city in silence. Athman asked me, "Do you want to go back home to the waiting arms of your dog or go out for a drink?"

"First of all, no more jokes about my dog. And what kind of drink are you talking about?"

"I know a nice club. We can stop there first, and then I'll take you back to your dog."

"You hang out in clubs?"

"Yes. Why? Shouldn't I?"

"But they're prohibited, dirty."

"Toilets are dirty too. You don't pray in them, but you still have to use them. It's the same with clubs."

"I don't understand anything anymore."

"I'll explain."

He went down some back streets I barely recognized, toward a run-down industrial section recently renovated by the artist community which was now the trendiest night spot in the city. We ended up in front of a jazz club, the Daddy-O. Athman rang the bell, a black security guard opened the door and greeted Athman with "Hey, Batman!"

"Hey!"

He was more famous in this club than the real Batman. He whispered to me, "One syllable makes the difference between Athman and Batman, and changes your whole moral outlook. You'll see what I mean! But don't worry, it's part of a plan."

We headed toward a counter where a tall, strapping Pakistani greeted Athman with a big smile and a "same as usual?"

"The usual, may God forgive us, and bring one for my friend."

The server put two beers in front of us. Athman, expecting my hesitation, winked at me and said, "Pick up your beer and act natural. You've become an over-eager novice at the idea of repenting. Hold on to your American side; it might come in handy. . . ."

We picked up our drinks without paying; it was the Pakistani's treat. We wound our way through the crowd and looked for a table away from the speakers in the smoking section because I hadn't had a cigarette since we arrived at Jamal's. Once we sat down, Athman said, "Don't worry. It's non-alcoholic beer. The Pakistani is in on it. Lots of people here know me, so they need to see me drinking from time to time. . . ."

I lit a cigarette and the first drag made me dizzy. And then to top it off, Athman couldn't stop with his preaching. Even lodged in the belly button of the devil, he will go on and on explaining Islam.

"The actual practice of religion is the least important part. Religion is not like exercise, it's doctrine, a thought process, the history of men with God. It's what enlightens us when everything becomes dark, and when everything is dark, one must never make a mistake about who the enemy is, and the enemy today is not those who don't say prayers or don't keep Ramadan; the enemy is elsewhere. He is powerful and rules the world, but it is God and God alone who should rule the world, not anyone else. These *Taghuts* have to be surrounded. Obviously, for the moment, they can't be overpowered, but you have to provoke them and see how they act. We have to force them to suffer their contradictions like ulcers and wear them down."

"I don't like non-alcoholic beer. It's the alcohol that makes the bad taste of the beer tolerable. I don't really drink, but if I'm going to drink something that tastes like beer, I want the real thing. Without the alcohol, it's just lying to myself, and I can't stand lying to myself."

Athman gave me an ironic look and said, "As for me, I'll keep on lying to myself. You hold on to your truth if you want."

He called the waiter over and ordered, "One beer with and one without."

Then he launched back into our discussion. "As I was telling you, they have to be attacked at the heart of their contradictions."

"The power is there to be able to attack other powers. If there aren't other powers to attack, then they attack themselves. We have to let them self-destruct. Attacking a superpower mainly does them a great service."

"You don't understand anything. Westerners hold the power to decide, to act, and to judge. They have all the dominoes, and they can block the game whenever they want. That's why it's not a good idea to play dominoes with them; they'll always win."

"That's just what I was saying."

"As for us, we'll play Russian roulette. You have to terrorize those who terrorize you. That's the only way to find an equal footing. That's precisely why only we Muslims can think differently from them. Don't forget it was because of us that communism got wiped out in the world. We can do the same with the Americans and their liberal capitalism."

"But that's about politics, not religion."

"They make the distinction between politics and religion because their religions are so limiting. By contrast, Islam is complete; it's tautological. Islam is a religion integrated with politics, and the politics that tell the truth are religion. For us, the political is both a step in the process and a strategy. At the end is Islam. Have patience! In my family, we say, 'Patience is the strategy of those who have no choice.'"

"But a religion that needs politics is no longer a religion."

"To them everything is Judeo-Christian. In its essence, Islam came in order to show these two religions that they were too shallow and incomplete. But they refused to understand. . . ."

"Calm down! Not so loud. I'm not deaf, you know. Everyone will hear us."

"They're all drunk. They can't hear a thing. If they had been listening, they would have heard it at the UN, when they were sober. It's not at the bottom of a bottle when they're already loaded that they can get to the bottom of the matter."

"You're really dreaming. Look at Algeria, where even an army as corrupt as the Algerian army can infiltrate Islamic underground networks. We won't all of a sudden become any smarter facing Americans."

"If they are stupid enough to get caught by that army, it's because they haven't understood anything about Islam. If you can't figure out how to draw enough energy and intelligence from the Koran to sustain you in combat, it's either because you don't know how to read the Koran, or because you're not smart enough to read it in the first place. If that's the case, then you should be content to surrender yourself to God and not put yourself in the position of God's combatant. Everything is right there in the Koran, but God challenges you to find what you're looking for."

The discussion was interrupted by the arrival of three nearly hysterical girls who threw themselves at Athman, while he kept them at a distance under the pretext of wanting to introduce them to me.

"Here are Aileen, Marie, and Selena!" he said pointing to each one. Then he whispered to me, "The last one's Jewish. I'd recommend Aileen; she's easy and great."

He invited them to join us, keeping Marie and Selena close to him and pushing Aileen toward me. Aileen began by asking me how I knew Athman, what I thought, what I liked, etc. Basically, she was trying to get through the boring part of the "approach" before we got to bed. After a minute, Athman asked the other two to follow him onto the dance floor. He left me alone with Aileen, who moved closer to me as an excuse to hear me better in such a noisy place. She somehow managed to launch into a discussion about abstract Arab art. She proceeded to tell me how since figurative representation was forbidden in Islam for religious reasons, Arab painters developed a style based on the arabesque and geometry. . . . She was knowledgeable about this and spoke quietly with great composure, as if each word she pronounced transported her. In the shadows I had trouble making out her facial features or the color of her eyes. But when she rested her head on my shoulder, she smelled like the earth, even in this smoke-filled room. When I pointed that out, she replied, "You got it! I'm a ceramist."

With that, she kissed me. That clinched the evening for her, and Athman had disappeared. The bar announced last call. I got up and said, "I have to find Athman."

"Don't worry, Athman is far away by now. The two girls he left with only sleep together. He's probably hot into it with them."

"But how I am supposed to get home?"

"I live close by. Come up for one last drink, and then we'll figure it out."

"That Athman is such a jerk, leaving me behind like this."

"If leaving you here with me means being left behind, then thanks a lot!"

"I said that just on general principle."

"After midnight, there are no more principles. There's only desire."

She clung to me, and with my arm around her shoulder we left the Daddy-O. We crossed several tiny alleyways that seemed more like hallways lined with long red brick walls which hid old factories with two floors renovated. On the first and second floors were the studios; the third floor housed offices with windows, each topped with an arch painted white. The frieze that divided the floors was also painted white. On the outside, the metal fire escape was black.

Aileen lived in one of these buildings. She turned half of a floor of what was once a shoe factory into a loft of nearly 3,000 square feet. In the middle she had one of those outdoor toilet units and a shower stall set side-by-side. Together, they formed a room divider between the work space and the living space. The main entrance was on the studio side which contained two kilns, a work table, and a clay bin. The apartment side was divided in half by a table and four chairs. The kitchen was on one side, the bed on the other. To create a more intimate sleeping space, the bed was a four-poster with thick curtains made of a cheerful floral pattern.

Aileen undressed and poured two whiskeys. She stroked my glass against her pelvis and then handed it to me. It was her way of attacking straight on at point-blank erotic range.

I stood up to take off my jacket, and Aileen took over by undressing me the rest of the way. She asked me to keep standing in the nude while she proceeded to kiss every inch of my body from head to toe. I thought it might be a sculptor's thing, or maybe as a student she had fantasized about a model and was now in the process of getting it out of her system before dealing with the present. When she got to my lips, she swooned and I felt her sink into my arms. Then I dragged her onto the bed, we got under the covers, and she pressed up against me. She was shivering from the cold, her teeth were chattering, and she was literally sweating icicles. I thought maybe that's what frigid meant, and that Aileen was the real thing. Between tears and fever, she explained, "It's always like this. I can't do it; I freeze up. If you force it now, it will really hurt."

"Take your time. I'm in no hurry. . . . In any case, I'm not in such great shape either. I'm more aroused out of nervousness than desire. . . . Just keep talking to me."

"When I get like this, I can't do anything at all."

"Do you know what causes it?"

"No. No doctor understands. . . ."

Her narrow hips made her look androgynous. She was thin with small breasts, curly black hair which framed her face, and big green eyes. Her fingertips caressing me transmitted exhilarating sensuality, and their electrifying effect filled my body with incredible energy. I could tell that her body was emptying and freezing up, she gave of herself to the point of hypothermia. I held her tightly and tried to warm her up, then we fell asleep, worn out by disappointment and alcohol.

Faisal was waiting for us at the Maimouna Agency. Athman handed him Jamal's business card. He checked the computer listings and said: "We have five vacancies. It would be best for you to visit them firsthand. There's one a hundred yards away from where Mr. Athman lives."

"Let's start with that one," Athman said immediately as he looked to me for approval.

"If you want . . ." I said.

Faisal preferred to take his own car because he was very afraid when someone else was behind the wheel, and because his insurance would cover all the passengers, while Athman's insurance would only cover him. This situation made Athman laugh.

"If insurance weren't required by law, I wouldn't have any. It's crazy. It doesn't make any sense to be insured against accidents and natural disasters. God imposes His will whether it's a natural catastrophe or an accident. And then you go and ask to be reimbursed for that! Man can't restore what God has destroyed. Let them try to put the earth back in place after an earthquake, restore life to an accident victim on the interstate, or reconstruct everything after a tornado! Taking out insurance against acts of God is really like trying to take a shower with a glass of water."

Faisal was a bit effeminate. With his skin smooth and taut like a baby's, he looked like a closet homosexual, or at least a latent one. Surrounded by such fervent Muslims, Faisal didn't know which God to turn to. But since he knew perfectly well which God mattered to those around him, he would agree with whomever spoke. But he would always try to say what he thought. "I agree with Athman. Insurance is ridiculous, but after all, we are a rental agency, so we are required to follow the rules. . . ."

"That's for sure. Those are the rules of the unbelievers," concluded Athman.

As soon as we got to the neighborhood, Faisal called the building manager on his cell phone to say we were coming. At the entrance to the building there was a wimpy Asian guy. He tried to greet us respectfully, but he mixed up a Buddhist greeting with the Islamic bow. He sashayed his way to the elevator, and when we reached the second floor he showed us a magnificent furnished one-bedroom apartment.

"Does someone live here?" I asked.

"No. All of the apartments are like this," replied Faisal.

I leaned toward Athman and whispered, "I can't afford this. I think we're in the land where the managers are ultra skinny and the apartments are ultra plush."

"Just take it. It won't even cost you the price of a studio."

"Are you sure?"

"Absolutely!"

Faisal suggested that we go see the other apartments. I said without much enthusiasm, "Honestly, I can stop looking right here. It goes far beyond my expectations. And besides, I would be Athman's neighbor. What will it take to finalize the lease?"

Faisal explained: "I'll prepare it and then you can work out the rest with Mr. Jamal. All I need is for you to fill out this information sheet."

As soon as I filled out the form, Faisal handed me the keys and said to the manager, "From now on, he lives here."

"Yes Sir, yes Sir," said the Asian.

With the keys in my pocket, we returned to the office to pick up Athman's car. He turned to me and said, "You'll move in two days. In any case, you'll only bring your personal belongings. For rent, you'll pay a nominal monthly amount that Jamal will set, but you'll also have a regular lease with the actual price of this apartment so that you can prove that everything is aboveboard: rent, security deposit, etc. Jamal will draw up all the papers so that you'll be legal."

"It's crazy how simple everything is. Quick and easy. Now comes the hard part."

"What's that?"

"Leaving Keytal and Jenny."

"Do you know why it's hard? Because you still have doubts. You're not sure what binds you to them, and you're not sure what it is that pulls you away from them. If love is not intrinsic to your beliefs, your faith is weak. There is no such thing as love without faith, and you can't put your faith in a woman and a dog. That's where secularism takes you: to loving cats, dogs, provided that you don't love God."

"Athman, there you go again! Every time you solve one of my problems, you manage to immediately tap into another one of my anxieties!"

"The solution is faith. Either you have it or you don't. I'm within God; you're within Shakespeare. I'm in the divine; you're in the tragic. I stand up vertically; you lie down horizontally. Nietzsche said: 'Tragedy is when those below don't know, and those above can't go on anymore.' For us Muslims, the one above can always go on: it's God. Those of us below must always know it. There's no such thing as tragedy in Islam."

He turned on a CD of the Koran as his way of concluding. Around seven in the evening he dropped me off at my mother's and said, "See you tomorrow at work. And have a good night with your dog."

"Enough talk about dogs!"

"I thought this was about love. Good night."

My mother wasn't at home. She hadn't said anything. I turned on my cell phone which Athman had forbidden me to use in his presence and found her message which said, "I wasn't feeling quite right this afternoon. I'll be at the hospital overnight. It's nothing serious. I love you."

There was also a message from Jenny who had probably been informed by my mother.

My mother's hypertension seemed to have gotten worse since my father died, but she didn't want to admit it to me. I was worried and called the hospital immediately. Dr. Ahmed Houry, a Lebanese friend of my father, reassured me by explaining that she had a nosebleed, which was a typical symptom for her, and that he was keeping her overnight in order to run some tests. He added that there was nothing to worry about. I told him that I wanted to come to see her right away, but he reiterated that it wasn't worth it and that it might tire her out just when she needed to get rest. He reassured me again and passed the phone to my mother.

"It's not serious. Don't worry. Open the fridge, there's a little tabouleh left. You can grill yourself a steak and thaw out the fries. There's yogurt, but I didn't buy any beer because it was too heavy to carry. It'll be delivered tomorrow. I love you, son. See you tomorrow."

She hung up before I could get a word in edgewise. She did it on purpose, because she hated answering questions about her health when she wasn't feeling well.

I made my dinner according to her instructions and then sat down in front of the television to watch the evening news.

The thought of Aileen brought a warm feeling all along my body. I wanted to see her again. When I left her just this morning her eyes were awash with desire, her hair disheveled, and her body warm. Even if we didn't make love, it was as if we had. She kissed me for a long time as if to apologize for her frigid response. I called her cell phone, but got her voice mail and then didn't know what to say. Then I called Jenny, who was at home.

"Where were you? We've been trying to get in touch with you for the last twenty-four hours!"

"I'm at my mother's. I know what happened and I talked to her at the hospital."

"You could've warned me yesterday that you weren't sleeping home."

"I haven't had a minute to myself. . . . Sorry."

"You're really not well. I don't know what you're up to, but I'm having a hard time understanding."

"There's nothing to understand."

"You don't want me to meet you at your mother's then?"

"No. I prefer to be alone. I'll call you tomorrow."

"All right, good night."

"Same to you."

Jenny hung up because we weren't used to this kind of situation. I had never been two-faced with Jenny, nor she with me. I felt, at that moment, a painful choice that I wasn't expecting: keep up my life as it was, not especially happy at that, or leave it in search of an identity which brought me closer to my dead father. I was looking for this identity with typical American drive and determination, which fit in with other values. I was experiencing the whole thing as an essential, life-defining dilemma, and Jenny saw it as a temporary imbalance. Given this difference of perspective, all we could do was hang up.

After three months of private lessons in Islamic theology given twice a week by Jamal and finished off every day by "politics in Islam" according to Athman, Jamal determined that I was ready to present myself at the mosque to ask for repentance. I was supposed to request it publicly after the Friday prayers. On two consecutive Fridays, I endured the silence of the imam and his faithful. The third Friday, I had a meeting with Jamal to go to the mosque with him.

Jamal opened the door for me. He was closely shaven with a touch of aftershave, and dressed in a shirt as white as in a laundry detergent commercial. As he kissed me, he caught a whiff of tobacco on me. "I told you to abstain from smoking, at least this morning. Cigarette smell immediately makes a bad impression."

"The craving was too much."

"You want to repent and you can't even control this craving?"

"Wait until he accepts my repentance and then I'll quit after. This is the third Friday that we've come, and the imam still hasn't deigned to see me."

"And if he decides today, your smoker's breath will turn him away."

Jamal was silent for the whole trip to show his disapproval. We trudged on in silence through the end of winter's mud in front of the fogged-up shop windows. I was as excited as a kid at *Eïd al-Adha*, when the joy of the holiday intermingles with the nervous apprehension about seeing a sheep's throat cut. This kind of fear imbedded in joy is the thrill of the holiday. The thought of going to the mosque and hearing and seeing the sheikh accept my repentance was the source of this exhilaration. At the end of a shop-lined street, we crossed at a stoplight where we entered a residential neighborhood made up of identical small houses with little fenced-in yards. The mosque was in the middle of this residential neighborhood, right where a food store had been. Jamal told me that in order to prevent Muslims from putting in a mosque the neighbors pooled their resources to try to buy the property and make a garden out of it. But thanks to God, it turned out that their bid wasn't as high as our faithful's bid. Since the mosque's construction, a lot of owners sold out to go elsewhere and the neighborhood's land values dropped by 40 percent. There are two ways to analyze the situation: either everything gets cheaper when God appears, or wherever Arabs move in, property values drop to nothing. This is the kind of ambiguity, Jamal said, that needed to be cleared up!

In the first room just off the mosque's entrance, we changed and took off our shoes. Jamal put on his gandura and skullcap, then we headed toward the pool of water for our ablutions. On the first floor was the rather small, tiled, square prayer room with a square-based pillar in the middle which connected to a ceiling shaped like a plaster parasol engraved in brightly colored and gold-encrusted arabesques and writings from the Koran. The overall effect was that of a kitsch which Jamal abhorred. At first, I thought it was for reasons of taste, but no, it was for religious reasons.

"The least decorative prayer rooms are the ones preferred by God and the most frequented by the angels," he explained.

I was leaning against the "pillar of penitents" as I had done for the last two Fridays. I waited seated, dressed in my suit, watching the others pray.

On this particular day, a young man of about twenty joined me, taking a place on the other side of the pillar.

At the end of the prayer after the *Fatiha* and the imam's sermon, I reiterated out loud my request for repentance three times in a row:

"I repent, O God! I repent, O Muslims! I repent!"

The young man next to me said his request for repentance in English. Apparently, he didn't know Arabic. I couldn't help but think that he was going to have serious difficulties repenting in a faith with "subtitles."

Jamal stood up and walked toward the imam. Kneeling in front of him, he spoke to him. I knew that he was pleading my case. When he had finished, he kissed the turban of the imam and returned to his seat. The imam called for me: "You who ask to repent, what is your wrongdoing?

"Ignorance."

"Are your parents Muslim?"

"Yes!"

"Did they leave you in ignorance?"

"No!"

"So where does your ignorance come from?"

"From my negligence."

"What did you neglect?"

"I neglected the Hereafter of my death and I sank into the Here and Now of my life."

"And why do you wish to repent?"

"To find the straight path, and strengthen the ranks of my Muslim brothers."

"Do you know the terms of repenting?"

"Yes!"

"Repent now in the presence of witnesses."

"O you, my Muslim brothers! Before you I repent! O God, I repent!

'I renounce my disobedience and my negligence.

I regret having been so disobedient, so negligent.

I pledge never to stray from the straight path and out of your ranks.

I give up my former life as I gave up the milk of my mother.

"O God, I repent! O Muslims, I repent!

'Praise to You, You the Sovereign of the heavens, of the earth and of all within it. Praise to You, You are the Truth, Your promise is a truth, Your encounter is a truth, Your word is a truth, Paradise is a truth, Hell is a truth, the Prophets are a truth, Muhammad is a truth, the Hour is a truth. O Allah! To You I surrender, in You I believe, of You I ask assistance, to You I return, through You I struggle, from You I accept

judgment. Forgive, then, the sins I have committed, what
I have hidden, and what I revealed. It is certainly You
who move forward and backward, there is no divinity
but You.'"

"Do you know the Witnessing of Faith?"
"I witness that there is no god but God alone, the
Unique, and that Muhammad is His Prophet."
"Do you know the opening Sura of the Koran?"
"Yes."
"Recite it."

"IN the name of God the All-Merciful. . . . Praise
be to God, Lord and Master of all worlds. The
Compassionate by essence and by excellence.
King of the Day of retribution. You alone we
worship and from You we implore help. Guide us
on the straight path, the path of those whom You
have touched with Your grace, and not of those
who have incurred Your anger, nor those who
have gone astray." (S1)

"Do you know the sura of the unbelievers?"

"SAY: O you unbelievers!
I do not worship what you worship!
And you do not worship what I worship!
And I shall not worship what you worship!
And you are not disposed to worship what I worship.
To you your religion and to me, mine." (S109)

After my recitation, the imam asked the advice of those present. "O Believers! This young man came to ask for God's forgiveness and you are his witnesses. You are not judges, because God is the only Judge, but you are responsible for his faith and the sincerity of his repentance. You heard him, you saw him, and you had the possibility of learning all about him. That is why I ask for your advice and I ask you the question: do you find him sincere? Do you accept his repentance?"

The majority of the faithful responded in chorus, "*Amin*," and the imam continued:

> "SAY: O my servants! You who have committed excesses to your detriment, despair not of Allah's power of forgiveness. Allah pardons all sins for He is the All-Merciful and All-Forgiving." (S39, V53)

"Perhaps there are some among you who hesitated to accept this man's repentance. To those, in order to calm their heart, soften their hardness, and quell their doubts, I recall the teaching of our ancestors: the imam Ibn Taymiyya taught us that repentance is required. God said to us,

> 'ASK forgiveness of Your Lord and then return to Him.' (S11, V3)

> 'RETURN repenting unto your Lord! Surrender yourself to Islam before punishment is upon you, for later you will not be helped.' (S39, V54)

"Our Raouf has committed no sins, neither great nor small. He was ignorant, being born of Muslim parents who lost their way as a result of their exile. Their son managed to keep a tiny Islamic spark burning deep within his soul, a spark he was born with and which today has lit the way for him to our mosque. Raouf is not a sinner; he's a lost soul who came to our door asking for forgiveness. O you Believers, accept him, welcome him, guide him. Our Prophet tells us: '*If humans didn't make mistakes, Allah would have created other human beings who would sin, so that He could forgive them. For He is the One who pardons, He is All-Forgiving.*'

"Dear Believers, God loves those who come back to him. It is said,

'I pardon fully the one who repents, believes, does good, and follows the right path.' (S20, V82)

"Repentance is first and above all the path of the Prophets since Adam, the first of our Prophets. It is said,

'ADAM received from his Lord the language of repentance, and God pardoned him. He is the Compassionate and All-Merciful One.' (S2, V37)

"Abraham:

'LORD! Make us into Muslims and our offspring into a Muslim nation. Show us the rites and accept our repentance. You are the Merciful One above all.' (S2, V128)

"David:

'DAVID understood that we only wished to test him. He begged forgiveness from his Lord and he bowed down in repentance.' (S38, V24)

"Moses:

'HE said: My Lord! Forgive me as well as my brother and make us enter into Your mercy.' (S7, V151)

"Jesus repented by answering God who questioned him:

'ALLAH said: O Jesus, son of Mary. Was it you who said to men: Take us, my mother and me, for two divinities apart from Allah? Jesus said: Glory to You! It is not my place to declare what is not the truth. You would have known it, if I had said it. You know what is in my soul and I know not what is in Yours. In truth, it is You who know the invisible worlds.' (S5, V116)

"That's how Jesus retracted everything that the Christian faith today is based upon. Their prophet, Jesus, repented to God, and they don't know it. They continue to believe in a Jesus gone astray.

"About our Prophet Muhammad's repentance, God tells us,

'GOD indeed accepted the repentance of the Prophet, the emigrants, the Ansar, and those who

followed him in the difficult times when the hearts
from a group of them almost slipped into error.
He is forgiving and kind.' (S9, V117)

"Thus, we can see that the Prophets, all the Prophets, have asked God for pardon and have repented. Our
Prophet repented in these terms: *'Lord, pardon me and accept
my repentance. You are He who pardons and He who accepts
repentance.'*

"It's difficult to admit that the man chosen by God to
be His messenger repents. That's the very humility that
makes the Prophets great. To finish, I will tell you the story
from Abu Sa'id al-Khudari:

'A man of unusual coarseness and violence, after having lived
his entire life in sin, one day asked that the most pious man be
pointed out to him. A mountain hermit was pointed out to him.
He went to see the hermit and asked him the following question: "Is there a possibility of repentance for me?"

The hermit, knowing the man, answered without hesitation: "No!"

So the man killed the hermit, adding yet another crime to his
sins. Then he went to ask who the wisest man on Earth was. A
person was pointed out to him, and he went to find him and
asked: "My life has been nothing but sin. Is there a chance of
repentance for me?"

"Yes," answered the man, "there is always the possibility of
repentance and no one can come between you and your
repentance except God."

After a silence, he advised him to go to a land that he
showed to him: "Over there is a land of goodness," he told him,

where "the people do nothing but fervently worship God. Go pray with them and never come back here since this is a land of misfortune."

So the man undertook the trip, but during the trip he died, overcome by exhaustion. The angels of mercy and the angels of punishment quarreled over him. One side said that he came as a repentant sincerely desirous of returning to God. The other said that he never did a good deed in his life and that above all he was a criminal. Then an angel appeared whom they begged for an opinion. He told them: "Measure the distance which separates the point where he left the land of misfortune and the distance that was left to him to reach the land of goodness. Then consider him as being in the place to which he was closer when he died."

The angels measured the distance and found that he was nearer to the land of goodness and sufficiently distant from the land of misfortune. Thus the angels of mercy took charge of him and he died repented.'

"My dear brothers, such are the lessons of our wise men. They teach us generosity and pardon. That's why we can say to Raouf he is a repented soul among his brothers, a Muslim among Muslims, and that he must make an effort to distance himself from the land of misfortune in order to come closer to the word of goodness.

'O Allah, You are my Lord, there is no other God but You. You created me and I am Your servant. I submit to Your promises with all my might. Beside You, I seek refuge from the evil I have committed. I give myself up to You who have bestowed benevolence upon me and I give myself up to You with all my sins. Forgive me, for none but You can forgive sins.'

"Peace be with you."

Following Jamal's previous instructions, I stood up at that moment, went to kiss the imam, and handed him ten hundred-dollar bills as an offering to support the mosque's charitable works. The imam had me sit down in front of him and asked God to forgive me:

"O Our Lord! Guide Your servants on the straight path. Open to them the doors of Your mercy, forgive them, that their sins may be absolved. Lead them on the path of repentance so that they may ultimately find paradise. For You are the Greatest and most Generous."

During the imam's *dawah*, I was overtaken by sobbing, with tears that seemed to well up from my fetal state. My tears had a taste that I couldn't recognize. It seemed I was making up for all of the tears I had never shed before, when I lacked moral conscience. I was behind in crying over my fate, which in itself hadn't yet caught up to my misfortunes. I didn't know where I stood in relation to these emotions that plunged me into confusion. I had never imagined that confronting ideas could be so overwhelming, that it could suck me into the whirlpool of all of my loves put together. I finally understood my father's refrain: "You shouldn't have ideas. You should have knowledge." My father protected me from ideas of fear, and all the emotions that went with it. Suddenly I felt like a poor example of a human being, which made me feel ashamed. What was I truly capable of?

What feeling of solidarity? What kind of sacrifice? What kind of self-sacrifice was I capable of? I was thirty-one years old, and I had no idea.

On leaving, Jamal congratulated me. "Thanks to God," he told me. "I'm so happy for you and for us. See you very soon. I've got to stay with the imam for a bit."

Several of the faithful came up to kiss and congratulate me. Athman took me by the shoulder. I was happy, relieved, but my reunion with God, with faith, felt more like perdition, so strong was the emotion. When I confided this to Athman, he answered me, "This is normal. You're at the point of convergence with your past life which is also the point of divergence toward your future life. Today you are at the very nodal point of the optical beam where the image is reversed. That's what gives you the impression of being at the same point, and besides, it's not just an impression; it's reality. What's changed for you is the direction of your sight. Your head was upside down, your feet skyward, and now you've got your feet on the ground and God in your head."

"It's amazing how everything is so clear for you."

"God is clear and loves clarity. Come on, I'm treating you to a *halal* meal from start to finish."

"Quit joking. It's an act of repentance, not a rite of puberty."

"For Islam, you're scarcely at puberty. So are you coming to the restaurant or not?"

"No, I can't. My mother is waiting for me."

Since her last medical checkup, my mother had gotten much weaker. She even asked for an extended leave from work.

For my mother to accept this, it had to be pretty serious. So I wanted to stop by to see her as soon as I could. Not wanting me to be bothered, she would say, "Come by whenever you can. I get out less and less anyway."

It was useless for me to tell her to try to get out more with friends or former assistants. She would give me the same old answer: "So many of them have retired far from here, and most of them have grandchildren which keep them busy all the time."

Now that was the killer innuendo as another way of saying: "I'm falling apart at the seams and I'm still not a grandmother, so what are you waiting for to get married?"

"You know, Mother, I've just come from the mosque where I went to pray and repent."

"What did you do, my son, that you have to repent?"

"Nothing. But until today I never considered myself a Muslim."

"God knows what you are."

"But *I* don't know."

"Why? Do I know who I am, my son? At a certain time in your life you have to stop asking questions about your identity so you can make yourself an identity. You have to let yourself live and then you'll know what you'll be. But you can't ever invent yourself without being something first."

"I wanted to get involved in my own religion, that's all."

"Religion is something which makes us, and which we live with, without thinking. The minute you start to think about it, that's when you've already lost it, my son."

She offered to buy me an ice cream at her favorite place nearby. She put on her coat and gloves and we went out arm in arm like in the good old days when we used to wait in the same place for my father to come home from work. My mother had, on general principle, forbidden my father to drink at home, except when we had guests who drank. And she couldn't stand it either when he'd go out drinking with his friends, because she never knew when he would come home or in what state. Since she was a "ritualist" at heart, she created the after-work meeting ritual at this restaurant. I would come home from school and she would arrive home before my father because her commute was shorter. Then we would go out to the restaurant to wait for him. He would park in the lot and meet us for his before-dinner drink. Then we would go home to eat dinner and go about our own business before going to bed. That's how my mother took control of my father's drinking. She used to always say, "The best way to get rid of a bad habit is to create a good one that can incorporate the bad one. In time, it'll become a good one."

At the restaurant she ordered coffee and even though I adored rum raisin ice cream, I ordered a scoop of chocolate and one of vanilla. My mother was surprised at my change in tastes. I told her it was a change in perspective.

We laughed, and the way my mother looked at me as I ate my ice cream brought me back to the pleasure of childhood, with my ice cream mustache, drips on my shirt, and ice cream slobbered all over my face. She was so mesmerized in her enjoyment of watching me that she wandered off into a dream world. I never knew what she was dreaming about. She was absolutely silent and the weight of her silence blocked out all the noise in the place. She had the same look at that moment that my aunts and my grandmother used to have when they would come here on vacation. It was the look of a Lebanese tourist who takes in the superficialities of the modern world with the scrutiny of traditional curiosity. This look of my mother's concealed so many of her travels. She had a gift for self-reflection that allowed her to see herself in the world. Over time, the distances of exile and isolation turned her into her only reference point. She was both a person of change and an identity that remained constant. She was a country unto herself. It was this look of my mother's that made me understand that you never lose your original nationality. This look of hers is a law that many judges would have trouble interpreting. When I finished my ice cream, she slowly swallowed the last drop of coffee mixed with sugar at the bottom of the cup and asked,

"Was your ice cream good?"

"It's always good here."

"We've gotten used to thinking it's good here."

"Okay."

"So how's it going with Jenny?"

"She's okay . . . but as for the two of us . . . I'm not so sure. . . ."

"Are you sure it's not connected to your repentance?"

"It has nothing to do with it!"

"So where did you do this?"

"At the Hamza mosque."

"You could have chosen another. . . . You know, my son, exile makes us into foreigners and there's nothing more anonymous than a foreigner. This anonymity forces us to be secretive about our faith. Our real sin is, perhaps, to have been closet believers, almost ashamed of our faith. But that doesn't justify what we Muslims have become today: hysterical exhibitionists. Excess doesn't remove the stains of history just as erasures don't make for high quality writing. Your repentance belongs to you, not to the mosque. Listen to your inner voice, not to the loudspeakers. Even if you whisper, God will hear you. He's not deaf. . . . As for going to the Hamza mosque for that, that's complicating things . . . all the more so today when all mosques are not necessarily holy places. . . . Come on, let's go before it gets too late."

On the trip home, she said to me as if thinking aloud, "Did you go to repent all alone?"

"No. Jamal organized the whole thing."

My mother couldn't stand Jamal. When it came to him, she would go on forever, and there was no changing her mind.

"With all his bank accounts Jamal is sheltered from every material concern. Anyway, he'd never know what a material concern is. He has only metaphysical concerns. He's rich but he doesn't have the upbringing of a rich person. I think the hardest thing in life is to fill up your life when your bank account is full. Only the truly rich know the secret of it. Growing up believing that any desire that pops into your head can be realized is an ongoing danger for the uncultured like Jamal. Now, if he has faith, that's something else. . . . I'll tell you that in spite of everything even with faith, he'll wind up doing the religion harm with all his money because of his lack of a proper upbringing. . . . In science, there's a principle which holds that extremes converge, for example, the extremely cold and extremely hot both burn, the extremely fast ends up by being immobile, and thus extreme wealth and extreme poverty produce the same criminal behavior . . . and you, my son, have nothing of the criminal in you."

She added with a deep sigh, "The fact that your father is buried here made me reconcile myself to this land. It's no longer foreign to me. I will not be able to leave it without going into exile a second time, without killing your father a second time. So it is. . . . Exile rips out of you what you hold dearest in the world as a way of solving the problem of exile. I would like you to know that we paid the price, and now we have to live in peace with it. If I had let your father's remains go back to Egypt, it would have meant exile for you as well, you who were born here, who are an American by birthright. If I had not buried your father here, today you would have been exiled in your own country. Think about that when you pray."

She was on the verge of tears and the fact that she held back only reddened her eyes all the more. As she put her coat on, I went to pay the check. Then she invited me to share vegetable soup and *kefta* with her for dinner. While she reheated the leftovers, I set a nice table and watched the news on TV. The Intifada had flared up again and I thought of how Athman would be happy watching this.

Today I wonder how I was able to live without the religious culture of Islam. When I try to remember how I thought before and about what, I haven't the slightest idea, no memory whatsoever. I became an amnesiac of the void that used to be inside me. It's like with alcohol: at the death of my father a year ago, I stopped drinking during the forty

days of mourning, and after, I could never take it up in the
same way. Today I don't remember the taste of wine or whiskey, and I have no memory of what if feels like to be drunk.
It's as if my memory was converted more quickly than my
consciousness. Some things deep within me found their
place naturally, but many ideas and arguments persist in
trying to undo my faith. It's not the devil who distracts me
or plays tricks on me because he knows that I am a novice;
no, it's the purification that I can't figure out. . . .

I think that when you grow up in a religious family, your
parents prepare your subjectivity to accept the laws of religion as being objective. When you grow up, like me, in an
absence of religion, in the sciences, literature, and art, it's hard
not to be philosophical in the face of religious precepts and
dogma. Athman considers my questioning a lack of faith.

"Questioning oneself about what is in principle an answer, is to lack confidence in a doctrine, and this lack of confidence is only a lack of faith. To question everything at every
moment is a secular religion, the religion of the 'Godless,' and
it's their strategy for maintaining peace because a man who
answers questions with other questions is not about to act.
This is what creates immobility when ideas are in movement
but actions are frozen. You know what our Prophet teaches:
'Patience equals half of faith. Certitude is total faith.' Faith binds
you to certitude and prevents you from fleeing from action
which is an obligation toward God since one cannot act without Him. He is implied and implicated in all our acts. Action
always takes precedence because it implies and implicates
God. Action should in no case be aborted in midair for then
it's your faith in God that's left hanging."

III

For eighteen months I hadn't seen a movie or read a novel, and I didn't miss it at all. All my time was taken up with one word which consumed me and made me think only of my rebirth. Every weekend since my repentance, Athman and I would drive over 200 miles to go hear a sermon so that I could learn to recognize different schools of thought and appreciate different imams. Each time, he chose a sermon devoted to a specific issue.

The last sermon had as a theme "speech, act, and action." On our way there, Athman told me, "It's not only about repenting. You have to widen your knowledge all the more because your sin was ignorance. Apropos of ignorance, you really should settle up with Islam."

"Why? Are there dues to be paid?" I asked.

Athman burst out laughing and answered, "You sure turned into a real American. You think settling up means paying out! No. Settling up with Islam means that everything in your life should conform to Islam."

"For example?"

"For example, are you still with Jenny?"

"Yes . . ."

"I think you ought to start by breaking up with Jenny."

"Why would I leave her?"

"Quite simply . . . because she's Christian."

"I have a very hard time dealing with women, but Jenny is so quiet that I often forget she's there."

"But you're forgetting that it's a great sin."

"You must be joking. Jenny is so harmless that she can't ever be a sin."

"Raouf, Islam is a book which is applied and not questioned. We don't have any Kabalah. That's what makes us different from the Jews."

"But we have the *ijtihad*, if I've understood correctly."

"Sure, but the *ijtihad* is mainly concerned with showing how to understand and apply the sacred Book. In the Koran there is no mystery to clarify. The Koran is pure light. There is no hidden meaning, there are only clear precepts that man often has trouble applying. You've got to separate yourself from Jenny because she's not Muslim. Period!"

"You know, I was pretty far from being a Muslim too."

"I know, and if you intend to put yourself on the straight path, you need to do it fully. Sleeping in the arms of a non-Muslim and outside of the sacred bond of marriage is to commit one of the greatest sins."

"What can I say? In a few days I'll tell her everything and I hope that she'll understand."

"You've got it all wrong. First off, there's nothing for her to understand. You have to break up with her in the most direct and ordinary way. One good fight and it's over."

"But we've never fought."

"All the more reason for it. It'll be the first and last time."

"We talk so little that we don't have a chance to get into fights. Besides, she does whatever I say and loves everything I love. It's like she has ABS, always in control."

"Do whatever feels right, but don't get hung up over it. You're leaving her because you're becoming a Muslim. Here they prefer separation for psychological reasons rather than religious reasons."

"They're also psychological!"

"For them, psychoanalysis is deep, religion is superficial. Leaving a woman because you feel like living your religion would seem ridiculous to them. You're immediately seen as backward. And the way things are these days, that even makes you dangerous. Around here, you inspire confidence only if you reject your religion."

"Jenny is from a devout Protestant family, and these girls are hard to convince. And when they are convinced, they are hard to dissuade. If I try to explain to her that I don't love her anymore, she'll see it as her duty to convert me into her 'reborn' lover."

"You see the power of faith! Why don't Muslims have this power? Can you tell me that?"

"Besides the Bible, Jenny knows the Canticle of Canticles by heart. That's how she gets power and faith."

"What about the power of the 'quanticle,' like in quantum mechanics? Do you know it? That could be the power of our bomb! Each to his own 'quanticle.'"

Deep down I was persuaded that it wasn't a matter of God's will, but Athman's idea, and it bothered me. I'll grant that he was brilliant, and he was right on several points, but sometimes he would put himself too much in the place of God without realizing it. He explained to me that Muhammad had died "in Aisha's arms," and that was the reason why it was very important to have a Muslim wife — to be able to die in her arms. But who went to see how the Prophet died at this intimate moment with his wife? Only God could know that.

I stood up to Athman so he wouldn't think I was totally spineless. I defended my love for Jenny on principle but, in reality, I was pleading an empty case. Today I wonder where the connections with Jenny were that made us love each other. Oddly enough, she had become strangely distant from me. I couldn't even admit it to Athman; he would've thought that he had more influence over me than he had ever dreamed.

Wrapped in my raincoat, I saw that we were approaching a red brick mosque shimmering in the mist, enveloped in fog, in the middle of a green expanse. In my childhood memories I had only images of sun-blasted mosques, open to heaven and surrounded by desert, reeking of sweat circulated by the overhead fans. Finding this mosque heated with its odor of wet wool, I felt the change like a metaphor for the atmosphere of Islam which had changed climate. It was like a warning sign that the universality of Islam was endangered.

The mosque was bursting at the seams, but Athman had planned ahead. He had e-mailed one of his friends to save us two places next to him. I felt like I was trampling seated people. We prayed pressed against each other. We were bound together shoulder to shoulder. Everyone was there more to hear the imam's sermon than to pray. I even had the impression that the prayers were rushed through and that they were a kind of warm-up for the sermon.

The imam took the pulpit and inspected the crowd as if trying to assess the number present. He had a steely look in his eyes and a bushy beard, a wide face topped by a turban which was a historical composite taken from the Mamluks, Turks, and the helmet of Salah al-Din. He adjusted his turban gracefully, lit up his face with a sardonic smile, and intoned:

"Speech, act, and action. Oh, how these three words have been abused! Everyone speaks, everyone acts, and everyone takes action. But what is the real sense of these three words on which and from which our life Here and Now is constructed?

"Speech is the act of speaking. Act is the function of our body carrying out its will: I'm in the act of physically rising, walking. . . .

"Man has a certain power over his statements: he can say what he wants. But does he do what he wants? No! Because the carrying out of action requires parameters such as space and time, which are in the hands of God. At the moment when man decides to act, he needs God. Even when he has to act for God, he still needs God even more, and when he has to take risks for God, he needs him even more. Therefore, actions have a hierarchy based on how closely they are joined to God or, in other words, your faith has to match the level of the action you want to take.

'ESPECIALLY do not say of anything: "I will do it
tomorrow"[without adding] If God wishes it.'
(S18, V23–24)

"Thus, every action, however insignificant it may be,
must be attributed to the One who allowed it. Without His
permission nothing is done, or else it is done against Him.
Thus, the greater your action, the greater God's presence
and intervention will be.

"The more men's responsibility is great, the more their
acts are meaningful to their life and the more they need
to be closer to God. Unfortunately, in our own countries, the
Muslim countries, our political leaders are very far from God
in their acts and in their decisions. And to explain away this
distance, they invoke political responsibility. O Believers!
There is no political responsibility. It doesn't exist. There is
only one responsibility, the one of the Believer facing the last
judgment. The rest is really 'political' in the basest sense of
the Here and Now. It is also said:

"'AMONGST humans there are some who affirm:
"We believe in God and in the last judgment,"
though they are not really believers. They seek to
deceive God and those who believe, yet they deceive only themselves.' (S2, V8–9)

"'WHEN they are told: "Spread not corruption on
the earth!"' they say: "We are only reformers."
Yet they are the corruptors though they do not
know it.' (S2, V11–12)

"One can truly see, from this verse, that man is capable of expedient behavior, activities, and speech. In order to avoid this kind of infiltration into the ranks of Believers, God has decided to put the faith of each of us to the test. About this, God tells us:

'DID you think of gaining Paradise without having undergone the tests that others before you have? They were touched by disaster and poverty. They were so shaken that the Prophet and those who shared his belief cried out: "When will the help of God come for our victory? The help of God is surely near."' (S2, V214)

'ALIF Lam Mim. Do men think that We will let it be said: "We believe" without putting them to the test? We have already put their predecessors to the test. Thus God will truly know those who tell the truth and those who lie.' (S29, V1–3)

'DID you plan to go to Paradise without God knowing who among you fought [for His cause] and who patiently waited?' (S3, V142)

"But God didn't stop with the test of faith of simple Believers. He put His own Prophets to the test. For Believers, and especially Prophets, are threatened from all sides. Enemies will use all kinds of ruses and strategies. God put Satan on the Prophets' path in order to instruct, to test, and to teach them how to develop their vigilance, their patience, thus reinforcing their faith, for Satan is the CIA, FBI, Israel, and their like all rolled into one. May God protect us from them!

'WITH each Prophet we keep an enemy among the criminals. But your Lord suffices as guide and help.' (S25, V31)

'THUS for each Prophet we have created an enemy: diabolical demons and humans who, in their iniquity, inspire falsely embellished speech in one another.' (S6, V112)

"Abu Talib al-Makki says in his book, *Nourishment of Hearts*: 'Patience is one of the ways which lead to Paradise and spare you hell, for it was said to us: the route which leads to Paradise is paved with tribulation and the one to hell is carpeted with desires.'

"The Believer must demonstrate patience to deserve Paradise and repress all desires if he wants to avoid hell. We must submit ourselves to hardship and arm ourselves with patience to deserve the supreme reward: Paradise. We see and understand that Islam is education, devotion, vigilance, political activism, and combat. It's all of this at the same time. One submits oneself to God in order *to be*. For it is only under God's veil, under the wings of His Mercy and in the path of His Guidance that we can be greater than the great, richer than the rich, more cunning than the unbelievers and stronger than all of our enemies. Thus, our speech can become act and our acts can be transformed into action, thanks to God.

"But if our acts, our way of acting, are defined in the sacred Book, how can we determine our actions? How can we understand that God expects of us such and such an action? What guides us to recognize and accomplish it?

"To find the answers to all these questions, you have to understand the meaning of Guidance. What is Guidance?

"For each act of faith, Guidance stems from God. The Prophets are there to guide humanity on God's straight path. This means explaining Allah's teachings to the world and showing it in practice. After the final message transmitted to Muhammad by God, which put an end to all further divine messages, from the day that Muhammad, on God's orders, finalized the Koran during his last pilgrimage, the responsibility to guide all of humanity on the path of Islam falls to Muslims. And if we do not do this, we will have to answer for it on the day of the last judgment. This is the fundamental framework in which the action of every self-respecting Muslim who also respects his faith, his religion, his Prophet and his God, must be expressed above all. For such a Muslim there must be no other matter of urgency as important. It is in these words that God gave the essential orders to His Prophet:

> 'SAY: O people! Here is the truth come to you from your Lord! He who follows the right path does so only for himself. He who goes astray, goes astray only to his own detriment. I am not a guardian for you.' (S10, V108)

"Unfortunately, Muslims have gone astray. They have distanced themselves from this divine Light, and they no longer know where their path lies nor where lies the path of God. . . .

> 'So, have patience. The promise of God is true. Do not let yourselves be carried away by those who have no conviction.' (S30, V60)

"What the Muslim world lacks is the patience to remain true to itself. Muslims are impatient to want to be like others. They are 'carnivalized' in their morals, they rob their souls to sell their principles, and then they're surprised that the true believers come in secrecy and proclaim the beginning of the battle.

"What the Muslim world lacks is the example. It's atrophied and Muslims are stored away in history's deep freeze. The power has to be cut off in order to thaw them out. You've got to strike at conventional and nuclear power plants, at the very spot where the current is produced, to stop this freezing. You must be patient and serve as examples of the virtues of the Prophets. God said:

> 'So be patient in the example of the determined men among those sent.' (S46, V36)

"When the Prophets dream, they're truthful dreams, in other words, divine revelations. When Abraham dreamt that God asked him to sacrifice his son, he quickly understood the meaning of it and grasped the profound intention. When he awoke he summoned his son and explained to him

the situation unsparingly and without reservation. He said
to him:

> 'MY dear son, I saw in a dream that I was sacri-
> ficing you. It is to you to see what is to be done.'
> (S37, V102)

> 'HE [Ishmael] said: "Father, carry out the order
> that you received. You will find me, if God pleases,
> one of those that are patient."' (S37, V102)

"This is the answer that consecrated Ishmael, a child
among the most enduring Prophets, and he became a model
of patience for all Believers, because, in two sentences, he
proved that he had understood what God asked of his father
and what his father asked of him. 'Carry out the order that
you received.' With this sentence Ishmael said to Abraham
not to discuss the order, no matter the cost. Carrying out
God's request was the only important thing. Ishmael didn't
consider himself a victim. He accepted to be the object of
fulfillment of God's will, without flinching, without discussion and in total submission, not at his father's request, but
on God's order. Then he said:

> 'YOU will find me, if God pleases, one of those that
> are patient and will bear the test.'

"Abraham as much as Ishmael left it up to God, guided
by the same faith and the same desire to answer God's orders.

The father delivered his son to God, and the son offered his neck to his father. When the knife approached Ishmael's throat, God intervened because the test was fulfilled, even if the sacrifice wasn't completed.

> 'WE called out: O Abraham! You have believed in your vision! It is thus that We reward those that do good. It was a difficult test; We redeemed him [Ishmael] in exchange for a beast of significance to be sacrificed.' (S37, V104–107)

"We see that Ishmael demonstrated patience in his submission to God, and if we compare him to Yusef (Joseph), who is a model in his refusal to disobey God, we would be tempted to ask ourselves the question: Which of the two is the more deserving? Ibn Taymiyya says on this subject: 'Patience in obedience is more deserving than patience in abstaining from sin, because the value of obedience is preferable to the abstention from sin, just as patience for God is above patience by God, since the "for" is linked to God's divine character and the "by" is linked to His sovereign character.'

> 'O our Lord! Put your servants on the straight path and toward success, open unto them the doors of repentance so that they may enter Paradise, for You are truly the One who sees and who knows all!'

"Peace be with you."

On the trip back, Athman was silent. He had cried during the sermon, and I had cried seeing him cry. We expressed our consolation to each other in the manner religion prescribed. Everything that transpired would have carried the weight of faith in a time of peace, but for Athman, now at war, the weight was that of faith, oath, commitment, and refusal. For him, the mosque no longer smelled of incense, but of *baroud*. After a minute, to break the silence, I asked, "What are you doing tonight?"

"And what about you? What are you planning to do?"

"I don't know. I feel like seeing Aileen again."

"But there's nothing to see in Aileen. She's a cold fish."

"She moves me."

"What do you mean?"

"She communicates feelings to me."

"When I go to see a woman, I have my own feelings when I go there, but you go looking to find them once you get there!"

"You're talking like a barbarian."

"Listen, if you don't get a hard-on thinking about a woman, you won't get it up when you see her either."

"It's more subtle than that."

"So, explain then: if a woman doesn't move you, you can't get it up?"

"That's right."

"Well, if I don't feel it before, I don't even go there. You would risk it. I don't see where the subtlety is."

"Let's end this debate right here! If not, I'm going to end up not knowing how I make love."

"Actually, that's not what I wanted to talk to you about."

"What did you want to talk about?"

"There's something big in the making and we've been approached about participating."

"Something big? Like what?"

"We're a long way from knowing exactly, but the need to do it is definitely in the air."

"What's our part in it?"

"To be martyrs for the cause."

"But that was obvious from the start."

"Obvious in theory, but now it's for real. We're on."

"I'll do it if it's worth it. I don't want to be a token martyr, but for the real thing, I'm on board."

"You have every right to think about it, if you want."

"It's the kind of thing you don't think about. As for me, I feel very committed. And you? What's your decision?"

"You know, the breeding ground for martyrs is pretty extensive. I think that this "action" requires some real scientific expertise, so right off the bat, many don't fit the profile. In my case, I said yes without hesitating because if real minds don't die for Islam, martyrdom will remain an idiotic idea for idiots. I think the fact that people like us agree to do it will change the scope of the problem. At least, that'll prove to them that what's important in Islam is the level of our faith, not the college level they give us. God said:

'THE noblest among you is the most pious in God's sight.' (S49, V13)

If they continue to believe that those trained in their universities run away from the idea of martyrdom, then we're participating in Islam's decline. They also have to understand that they succeeded in corrupting a lot of Muslims, but not all."

"Are you capable of dying in order to say all that?"

"Oh, yes, among other reasons."

"I'm telling you, I don't want to die for ideas."

"We're dying for God!"

"Okay, but that doesn't tell me how you want to spend the evening."

"I'm think I'll go see my wife. And you should drop Aileen. Don't forget, tomorrow we have a full day."

Athman came to get me, first to go to a horse race before heading off to a "militant meeting," to use his term.

Athman put in a CD of the Koran chanted by the great Koran reciter Abd as-Samad:

"WHEN God's victory shall come and the doors
     will open,
When you will then see people enter God's reli-
     gion en masse,
Proclaim the glory and praise of your Lord and
     pray to Him to forgive you;
He always accepts the return of those who repent."
(S110, V1–3)

Then the road opened up in front of us, both sunny and shaded at the same time at the summer's end. Athman stared at the asphalt as if it were transformed into a teleprompter and he was reading his thoughts on it.

We drove on in silence, carried away by reciter Abd as-Samad's virtuosity which set our breathing to the rhythm of the text, sweeping us away in emotions which protected us from our problems and identified their the source. This chanting took on a greater significance when Athman turned into a road in an oak forest. He told me, "You realize that there are no trees more twisted than oaks and olive trees. But God also made his straightened version of the oak: the larico or Corsican pine. They make boat masts out of those trees. It's the same for us, in the Koran, the most twisted can become straight."

"Is it still far?"

"We have the meeting in this forest. There's a private race track."

We arrived at a kind of ranch, whose owner was a young Saudi, a real equestrian enthusiast. He greeted us himself in the parking lot next to his house. He was muscular like a weight lifter. Dressed in jeans, a red shirt covered by a buckskin vest, spurred boots, and a bandana around his neck, he looked like he just stepped out of the movie *Rio Bravo*. He addressed us in Arabic, and the contrast between his language and his cowboy appearance was so great that I couldn't hold back laughing, all the more because it reminded me of my first vacation in Beirut at my grandmother's. With the neighborhood kids, we had gone to see *Spartacus* with Kirk Douglas, dubbed into Arabic. We must have seen the film a dozen times with Kirk Douglas, half-naked in his slave costume speaking Arabic with the accent of an imam, and Jean Simmons answering him "I love you" in Arabic, which had us all rolling on the floor laughing. The great American films dubbed in Arabic were for us the greatest comedies. Luckily, Athman immediately took charge of our host and moved in front of me. I followed them, trying to control my laughter by breathing in deeply.

The owner took us to a kind of raised deck next to his house which overlooked a racetrack. Jamal was there seated majestically on a chair that looked like a throne. While looking out through his binoculars, he explained to us, "This isn't a regulation course but a track for training racehorses and especially for being able to analyze the behavior of each one so we can adjust the training preparation. This way we avoid trying them out on real racetracks where they can be seen. If you want to win races, the less the competitors know the horses, the better."

After two races during which Jamal's horse performed honorably, two Asian women, veiled, came to serve us tea along with pastries which were still warm. It was exactly at this moment that Jamal explained to me that I was to accompany Athman to the sermon of an eminent sheikh whose name had, for the moment, to remain a secret. He added, "He came into the country with false papers. Because he's in hiding, he doesn't preach in public but, don't worry, it's all in order with God and that's what's important."

Getting back in the car Athman said to me, "We're going to follow Jamal. He'll lead the way."

After a few miles, we arrived at a parking area in the middle of a forest.

"Stop here and get in with me," Jamal told us.

Athman left his car and Jamal dropped us off a few miles further at an intersection with a covered bus stop. A few minutes later, a black SUV with dark tinted windows pulling an Airstream trailer stopped right in front of us. Athman knocked on the trailer door. A hooded man opened the door for us. Athman told him,

'DARE to wish for death if you are sincere.' (S2, V94)

The trailer was windowless and without decoration or furniture. There were only carpets on the floor. We took our places along with the dozen people already there. After half an hour on the road we got out at a kind of hangar, and took an interior stairway to a room as bare as the trailer. Four hooded men armed with AK-47s guarded the two exits, and two others were seated on each side of the sheikh who, at the nod of one of the guards, began his sermon:

"In the name of God the Merciful and may the prayer be over our Prophet, God told us:

'AND tell the Believing women to lower their eyes, to preserve their chastity, and not to display their beauty except what appears outwardly. Let them hide their bosom with their veil and let them uncover their beauty only to their husband or to their own father or to the father of their husband, or to their own son or to the sons of their husband, or to their own brothers, or to the sons of their brothers, or to the sons of their sisters, woman attendants, or to their woman slaves, or to male servants who feel no desire for women, or to boys who have no knowledge of the existence of the female private parts. And let them not stamp their feet to have their foot jewelry jingle to make known what ornaments they hide. Come back all you to God. O Believers, may you reap success.' (S24, V31)

"God tells the truth. All the religions that our Prophet recognized determine laws of modesty for women; Jewish women wear wigs so as not to show their hair, Christian women wear a 'veil' when they are nuns, and Islam calls for the hiding of anything that can pass as adornment for women. Does our religion call for something that is not recognized by the other Books? All the more so that God sent our Prophet as the last of the messengers to perfect the other Books. The Koran is the last Book which God in His generosity has consented to give to humanity.
"It is said:

'To you We have revealed the Book in its full Truth and justice to confirm what existed of the previous Scriptures and to protect them.' (S5, V48)

"In this regard, he confirmed with more clarity what already had been practiced in the other religions. Why accuse us today, as they do, of being more closed, of being sectarian and repressive when we are human beings faithful to God, and we want only to enforce the religion of God who told us:

'PROCLAIM aloud what is decreed to you and turn your back on the unbelievers.' (S15, V94)

"We want to live in the divine realm and follow the example of our Prophet. We are the faithful, and faith in God requires a conscience. To call us extremists is to attack our conscience and interfere with our inner life, with our spirituality as *Ummah*, as Muslims, as a people, as Believers who have accepted the last judgment. How do you expect us to listen to mortal and unbelieving men and not betray our faith?

'FOLLOW what is revealed to you and have patience until God judges. He is the best of judges.' (S10, V109)

"Our enemies believe that we have fallen into Islam as one falls into an abyss; you don't fall into Islam, you are reborn in Islam. Islam has descended toward those who were in the abyss in order to raise them up to spiritual values which teach them how to save their soul. Islam's enemies do not sleep and wonder why we are not sleeping. Islam's enemies do battle and wonder why we struggle. Islam's enemies are developing and advancing and do not wonder why we are going backwards and remain underdeveloped, because all the values they have created for themselves remain theirs alone. They won't let us benefit from them. This is why our duty is to return to Islam. It's our religion, our God which will give us modernity and prosperity, not the Christians or the heathens. For centuries their world has been evolving and ours has been going backwards. The proof of their evolution is seen in the caliber of our emigration. At the beginning of the century it was the slaves, at the middle of the century it was the workers, and at the end of the century it was the intellectuals, which means that from colonization to decolonization there has been a destruction of our peoples. And if we're at this point now, it's because we've abandoned our religion. We've dressed ourselves up in their image. The more you look like them, the more you become vulnerable. We must be what God tells us to be and we will become different, more and more foreign, so as to push them toward racism, to push them toward fascism, so that they become extremists in the defense of their interests. They have undermined our values; we have to undermine theirs. This is what God wants of us. And He tells us:

'AND say: 'I am He who comes to give distinct warning.' (S15, V89)

"No one can read the world from Antiquity onward with only one language. Universality is plural and oneness is God. From the dawn of time, they tried to understand the secret of the pharaohs but they didn't understand a thing. They tried to crack the secret of the Incas but they didn't understand a thing. Let them build a pyramid with the means available to the pharaohs or Incas, and that will prove that they are at least as intelligent as they.

"It's obvious that their culture is not universal, since it doesn't know how to read the civilizations of five thousand years ago. How dare they claim to have understood Islam and Muslims when we, Muslims, with the help of God and our faith, haven't come close to determining the immensity of God and His message, so lacking are we in piety, wisdom, and imagination to grasp the immensity of God's spirit. In

that, there is an allusion to the fact that the common hatred
they have for Muslims allowed them to overcome their differences. Past history proves it, and present-day reality confirms it. In this sense the Jews have historically been in
league with the idol worshipers, even among the *Quraysh*,
in order to wage war against Muslims.

"Today we are faced with the same conspiracies. The
world Jewish diaspora, international communism, and
Western Christianity all put aside their differences to unite
against Islam. Their language is one as soon as it comes to
fighting Islam. This confirms what the Koran says:

'THE unbelievers are joined together.' (S8, V73)

'THE wicked help each other.' (S45, V19)

"But our enemies aren't only the Jews and Christians.
They're also our own leaders, those who govern the Arab
nation, all its kings and presidents. It's because our leaders
have lost faith in God and believe in the microchip. They are
more afraid of accounting to banks than accounting to God.
They have lost faith in the justice of the message. They have
built countries without the foundation of the *sharia*. They
have gone into debt to satisfy their desires for luxury. They
have untapped our riches to enrich our enemies. They have
built places of depravity and prostitution instead of embel-
lishing God's mosques, for God is beautiful and loves beauty.
The heathens want to judge us by setting the devil up as judge,
while our faith requires God as the one and only judge.

'THE word of your Lord is fulfilled in all truth and in all justice. None can change His words. He hears all and knows all.' (S6, V115)

"My brothers! Soothe your hearts, thank God for his mercy, raise your hands to the supreme request. You are the best in the sight of God.

"Peace be with you."

The imam's oratorical talent was exceptional. He had succeeded in transforming the sermon, which should have remained a human word, a word to help the faithful solve their problems of the Here and Now with God's mercy, into an almost divine word which served to complete the word of God. With his charisma, he had expropriated this place of religious exchange as its primary purpose and transformed it into a place of political propaganda. This was doubly serious because the emotion in listening and the submission of the faithful were religious in nature. As we left, I said to Athman: "Don't you find it's a bit much? He's really political in his sermon!"

"We have been so massacred that the slightest grain of truth seems an exaggeration. He didn't say a thousandth of what there is to say. Look at yourself. You're discovering at the age of thirty-one that you have an ancestral religion you don't know. Is your ignorance due to chance or history?"

"Let's say that it's due to the winds of history."

"No, there is chance and bad luck on one hand, aggression, colonialism, and oil on the other. That we have oil is perhaps by chance, but that they came to take it certainly is not. You know, when I think about all this, my guts get so wrenched that I feel like throwing up from hate! The hate I have for them never leaves me. It's like my faith; it never leaves me either."

"What bothers me, what really annoys me, is that the more murderous the 'act,' the more it will shake them up, threaten them, and force them to think and push them to another level of awareness. They themselves are tired of being the absolute power; it scares them. Great powers are afraid of themselves so they need others to make them afraid so as not to risk destroying themselves," I said.

"Ever since the Crusades, they haven't stopped being crusaders. Now that they're at the height of their power, they have to recover this power at the expense of Islam, like they took back the power from Arab civilization for their own gain. And don't forget half of them will be with us, like the anti-globalization militants who don't really know how to destroy the system. It's up to us to do it for them. Whatever their might and power may be, you can make them fail using their own methods and your own faith. Reread the Koran and you will see that all during the Prophet's life, God didn't give him a powerful army but simply faith, thanks to which he was able to turn the enemy's power against itself. And you can do it too. Because what isn't yours by their rights belongs to you by God's rights. The enemy has exploited us through colonization to create all of today's technology. But we have to be ready to appropriate it for ourselves. That's God's justice. Instruments are only means in the service of all thought. Why not also in the service of Islam and its glory?"

"But you're talking like a Marxist!"

"Just between us, Marx isn't all bad. Pity he was a Jew and not a Muslim! On the other hand, to create all this technology, those in the West have developed endless inconsistencies in their societies, in their thought, in their religions, to the point that they've ended up admitting inconsistency as the basis for all reflection, processes, movement, and consequently, for all advances in thought, even to the point of being necessary to generate ideas," he replied.

"That's true! A society that doesn't know inconsistencies doesn't advance. It's dead."

"You see how you think like them! But their inconsistencies are their weak point. God is unique, but without inconsistency. God is peace and inconsistency is war. God is serenity and inconsistency is anxiety. God is tranquillity and inconsistency is worry. They accuse us of being fundamentalists and yes, we are! A Muslim must be fundamentally uncompromising when it comes to inconsistency. When that happens, purity has meaning, the absolute has meaning, and God has His place."

"You frighten me, and you annoy me, because you politicize everything!"

"Politics is the art of creating a structure for your expansion. In order to live your religion fully you need this structure, and as long as you don't have it, you're just plain political, period. I am really a politicized believer. . . ."

"I mean that you react obsessively when it comes to certain problems. Your hate, for example, is obsessive."

"If obsession is about not forgetting, then yes, I am obsessive."

"Obsession is when hate has nothing to do with anything, but you justify it all the same."

"You still really don't get it, do you? What does hate mean for you? Are you trying to make excuses for them?"

"All I'm saying is that hate is bad enough, so why make it worse? That's all I mean."

"And what do you hear them say obsessively here in America? 'America is a free country.' I want to be *as free as* America in my country, I don't want to be free *in* America. You get it? And it's also a question of acting, not just of naming the act. We can't afford to name our acts, because we don't have the institutions necessary to do it. So they call us terrorists. Do you know when I became a terrorist? When I was scarcely seven years old, my little sister was stuck under my parents' bed and I couldn't get her out. I think it was because her dress got caught on one of the mattress springs sticking out. When I got to the big living room where my brothers and sisters were talking and laughing, I tried several times to explain to one of them what had happened to my little sister but they kept ignoring me. My mother had put plates on the table for dinner. I took a plate and I threw it on the floor and broke it. Everyone fell silent, my father came toward me, grabbed me hard by the arm and said to me, 'What has gotten into you?' 'My little sister is stuck under the bed.' 'Your little sister is stuck under the bed and you go and break a plate? What does one have to do with the other?' At the age of seven I understood that the terrorist act is the one which has nothing to do with reality. But one which gets listened to."

"You're telling me to break plates?"

"There are some who have a lot on their plates, and we'll be the ones to break them!" he concluded with a chuckle.

Jenny loved Indian cooking. She adored curry, tandoori, and naan. I had invited her to our favorite Indian restaurant on campus where for the first time we had decided that we were going to live together. I was confused. How was I going to announce that I was breaking up with Jenny? How could we separate when we really didn't feel like it, and when the reason for it had nothing to do with our relationship? And at the same time, I had no memories of anything resembling passion. If I had to tell her that we had to separate, I'd have to explain to her why I didn't love her anymore and, in order to do that, I had to know why I had loved her in the first place. Well, I just didn't know anymore. Breaking up because we're reevaluating the relationship could be a sign that the relationship is evolving. But breaking up without understanding what led to the relationship was a disaster. Maybe Jenny was like a trip whose point of departure I had forgotten and whose destination didn't interest me anymore, or in any case, I didn't understand. What I did know was that Jenny was anything but an end point. The maître d', who knew us, put us at our usual table. He remembered it because we had taken a lot of time in choosing it, and he had been amused by our indecision.

Jenny didn't suspect anything, and I didn't know how to bring it up to her. How could I lead up to the decision without giving her a lot of explanation? How could I convince her of a separation that I wasn't convinced about? How could I tell her when I couldn't tell myself?

She dug into the piping-hot naan with a sensuality that aroused in me all kinds of appetites. She spoke to cool off the pieces in her mouth: "I don't know in honor of what or for what reason we're here, but it's an excellent idea!"

"We're here because I've got some problems . . . there are a lot of things I don't know anymore."

The airy naan flattened out in her fingers. With her eyes wide open in amazement, she said to me, "So, what's the matter? The thing with Keytal is settled. So what is it now?"

"I don't know. I'm feeling really unbalanced right now. I'm having doubts. I'm feeling lost. . . ."

"Maybe you're depressed."

"No, it's not depression. It's like a change in direction."

"So where do you want to go?"

"I don't have any precise direction, but I have the clear impression that the road I've been on until now is the wrong one."

"What do you mean by a wrong road?"

"I mean I'm on a road which doesn't look like me."

"If you feel like changing your looks, it's not that simple."

"I'm trying to talk to you seriously, and you're making jokes about my looks!"

"I don't understand what you want to change: the direction, the road, your looks, or me?"

"There you go again! You make everything about you!"

"No, it's not all about me; I'm just making the necessary assumptions."

"Well, that's the end of that, then!"

Jenny took a deep breath, called over the maître d', and asked him to exchange her lamb korma for a steak and fries.

"What's gotten into you?" I asked her.

"It looks like we're in for a difficult conversation and I don't feel like ruining my lamb korma with it."

With a lump in her throat she lowered her eyes and stared at the last piece of naan on her plate. A drop of cold sweat rolled down my back. I felt like I was assaulting innocence itself. Was she the first victim of my repentance? I left it up to God. Why did she have to suffer? She was suffering all the more since her animal instinct was telling her that that I still loved her. God! It's hard to separate from a woman intellectually. She's not a Buddhist, God, she's one of the "People of the Book." Isn't there an exemption for the newly repented?

"What are you thinking about?" Jenny asked me.

"I don't know . . . about everything, about nothing . . . I'm not sure."

"So you announce to me that things aren't right between us and then you just drift off into space. Now, that makes perfect sense."

"I don't even know where to begin. . . ."

"Don't begin then, just give me the ending, the final score."

"We're over!"

"We're over? We're separating? We're not going to see each other anymore? We won't call each other anymore? We won't sleep together anymore? We're not going to eat together anymore. . . . You didn't tell me at what time the separation is due to go into effect."

"Listen, this is a serious discussion and you're not taking it seriously. . . ."

"I'm not taking it seriously? You forget that we've been living together for three years, we've been thinking about marriage for a year, my parents have adopted you, your mother adopted me, your father, before his death, had adopted me, and you just tell me between a naan and a korma that you're changing direction and you want nothing to do with me anymore? And for you, that means taking it seriously?"

"We're not going to get married just because our parents have adopted us."

"But it is important just the same."

"It's you I'd marry, not your parents."

"Granted, but if my parents approve, all the better."

"But we're not even there. . . ."

"Where are we, then?"

"I don't know. . . ."

The waiter arrived with the steak and fries for her and the lentil soup for me since I didn't eat meat in restaurants anymore unless I was sure it was *halal.*

Oh, screw it! I thought. Jenny had become nothing more than a piece of ass to me now. She was incompatible with all my life's desires and even more with my longing for death. She was physically bland like a passion without flavor that arouses no appetite. She was an empty act in a bleak world of anxiety. She was what's left of water in the desert, she was a salt water memory that increases thirst. What had happened inside of me?

I got up to go to the restroom where I dunked my head in a sink full of water. Wet down to the waist, I left the res-

taurant without even telling Jenny, leaving her to her steak
and fries.

I left the restaurant and like a robot headed straight for
Daddy-O's in the hope of seeing Aileen again. The Pakistani
guy was happy to see me. I asked him if he knew Aileen.
He smiled and whispered discreetly in my ear, "She won't
be long."

Then he served me a beer. I asked him: "With or without?"

"With."

"Well, cheers!"

I took my glass and I found a place across from the
entrance hoping to see her before she saw me. I waited for
Aileen, wrapped up in the feeling of how stupid I had become.
I had left Jenny like a cowardly, cynical deserter, or with a
cowardly cynicism, to run to another who froze up at the
thought of male contact. Maybe it was her way of extending
her life. As for my mother, screw it.

I think that I switched my normality like you switch
sidewalks. My head followed along as much as it could but
the remnants of my previous life didn't follow along at all.
The worst was that I had come to Aileen like you go to a
whorehouse, to a certain whore because she has a special
technique. Deep down inside I had an incredible longing to
make love, but I felt I would climax crying. I felt my tears
and my testicles united against me to the point that if I cried
right at that moment, I would ejaculate like a hanged man.
The two functions were interconnected. Like a computer, I
had a virus but no anti-virus patch. That's why Aileen at-
tracted me. I saw her in such a state that anything could

happen to me, without me having to worry about her. It wasn't disdain, but let's just say she made it easy for me to forget about problems, without feeling guilty. And besides, she had a great body and knew how to kiss, even if I had to wait for the morning. I was almost sure that once she put her arms around me, she would be superbly sensual. She had ruined so many nights that she could literally transport herself to seventh heaven all by herself, and I would only need to be there as a parachute for the landing. It was so painful for her to even get started that she must have needed a highly developed erotic imagination. It was no accident that she was passionate about Arabic abstract art and fascinated by arabesques. After one night with her, you could understand her choice of art, of kilns and clay. And especially the unpredictable aspect of the art of ceramics: the final result.

After my third beer I saw her come in. She headed straight for the bar and the Pakistani sent her over to me right away. I felt her coming toward me as if toward a fresh start, very happy to be waited for, which proved that it didn't happen often. Anyway . . . she kissed me very tenderly. She turned down my invitation to have a drink, and instead offered me a drink at her place.

As soon as we got into her loft, I ordered her to undress and get in bed.

"If you want a whiskey, I'm serving you!"

I poured two whiskeys while she got in bed. I handed her a glass before getting undressed and joining her under the sheets. She snuggled up against me so tenderly as to be literally aquatic. I was submerged in emotion. A gurgle at the back of my throat, so sugary that it made the nerves of all of my molars tingle. I clenched my teeth out of fear they would loosen, the hairs on my skin stood on end electrified and heightened my tension to the point of crushing my Adam's apple and silencing my tongue. I was liquefied without saying a word. She felt a warm tear on her forehead, and when her hand touched my penis I was ejaculating prematurely. My sperm flowed without contraction, without pleasure, and in pain. It was an overflow of distress. I spurted out my fear into the arms of a desperate girl who could find nothing better to say to me than: "Oh, too bad . . ."

My secretions had softened her caresses, her passion became more expressive and her longing unmistakable. My failure had set her free and I don't know what delirium led to finding her on me, full of me.

Yes! Elsewhere! Elsewhere! I wanted to cry elsewhere so my tears wouldn't come back. I wanted to cry tears, the best vintage tears of my childhood to intoxicate me with a life that was slipping away. I wanted to go looking within her for a birth source I could appropriate in place of absence. I opened her eyes to look into the whites of my death. I washed my face at her mouth and performed my farewell ablutions. She let out a moan from deep within, and released an aromatic breath, a candied perfume which satisfied my appetite for the human. She was in a trance. Celebration saturated our skin. I had come back from my absence. With a piercing orgasm she closed up like an oyster keeping my penis inside of her. It was impossible for me to pry loose from her. She asked me to slide slowly along with her on our sides so that she could relax and let me go.

What happiness to be caught in this trap, between pain and pleasure! To sleep with my penis in a prison worthy of it is to attain the deepest sleep in the nirvana of the sensual. I was dribbling from it like a nursling. She forced me into total immobility, and after a while I no longer knew if my penis was inside or outside of her. Our legs were intertwined in an uncomfortable static position. I had a tingling in my leg that fell asleep and I felt her leg as if it were a part of my own body. With bodies interlocking, we fell asleep inside of each other with the hope of remaining as two tomorrow, but devoid of sexual desire.

The next day I couldn't drag myself into work. In any case, the boss was a friend and, for a time, I had neither the mind nor the ideas to work.

Aileen liberated me from her hold at about four in the morning by peeing, and we both cracked up in a fit of laughter. She couldn't hold it any longer and luckily she had me in a tight grip because I too could barely hold it. . . .

A second later we got up. After turning on one of the kilns to warm up the place, Aileen made some coffee and we sat down for breakfast next to the kiln. I listened to her talk about art, color, clay, the firing, the research involved. . . . This kind of discussion late at night in a bar is fine, but it seems out of place on an empty stomach in the morning. I felt like I didn't understand English anymore.

Besides, I really felt incapable of carrying on a serious conversation about art and still less on a technical level. To change the subject, I asked her: "Do you like the U.S.?"

Surprised, she answered me, "Why? Did I say something against the U.S.?"

"No, not at all. It's just a question I'm asking, that's all."

"But I'm an American!"

"Me too."

"And you don't like the U.S.?"

"Sure, I like the U.S."

Aileen immediately picked up on our last conversation after serving herself some more coffee. In order to get her out of her monologue, I led her to a discussion on painting:

"I love paintings which treat religious themes. For example, Rembrandt's *St. Peter's Denial,* Leonardo da Vinci's *St. Anne with the Virgin and Infant Jesus,* Tintoretto's *Ascent to Calvary.*"

"Religion isn't my thing."

"You're not a believer?"

"I don't know what I am."

"And that doesn't bother you?"

"No! I live my art as an American, and that's enough for me in life and in the world."

"You're not at all a believer?"

"Even more than that. I was raised outside of any religion. My father is Armenian. He met my mother in New York and it's only when he fell madly in love with her that he found out she was Turkish. Love triumphed, so they got married but religion lost out. At home we talk about everything except God . . . it 'brings bad luck.'"

Aileen told me all this with a natural simplicity that made me burst out laughing, I don't know why.

"That makes you laugh?" she asked me.

"I've heard just about everything about God, but that He brings bad luck, I confess, that idea never crossed my mind."

"I don't know what it is."

"I think you're right. Let's talk art."

I spent the whole morning with her and then we ate in a pizzeria because she wouldn't have a hamburger.

At the end of the afternoon, Athman came to wake me from a replenishing nap.

"Where did you go? The Pakistani told me you saw Aileen again last night. Are you still wasting your time on that dog?"

"Why should this bother you?"

"Just when things are becoming serious, you're letting yourself get distracted? The first phase of the plan is decided and we have to pull away from everything and everyone for two months."

"What do you mean?"

"No more credit cards, no more checkbooks, everything in cash."

"Without a credit card or checkbook, how am I supposed to get cash?"

"You'll find an envelope in your mailbox every Friday with enough cash to allow you to live very comfortably for a week. No more cell phone, no more home phone, all calls are to be made from a phone booth, never the same, and especially not from the neighborhood ones."

"Okay, and for the rest?"

"The rest is simple! Jenny, over, Aileen over, and your mother, over."

"But my mother'll freak out!"

"You figure it out. Tell her you're leaving on a trip, that your office is sending you to Europe for some training."

"And when do we have to start doing this?"

"We have a week to take care of all our current business and especially to see that nothing shows up before five months' time."

"What do you mean?"

"You've got to take care of everything and arrange for everything to be put on hold, no appointments of any kind, for the next five months. You've got to make it look like you've disappeared while still being here."

"And work?"

"We'll work for another two weeks as normal. After, in the office, we'll be assumed to be away on business."

"My mother'll be a big problem."

"Don't worry, everything'll be all right with your mother."

"Easy for you to say!"

"Trust me! Okay, come on, tonight I'm taking you out to eat. I know a great Pakistani restaurant!"

"Please, anything but Indian or Pakistani. . . ."

"How about Moroccan?"

"If you want. . . . But I really feel like McDonald's."

"Over my dead body!"

Telling my mother that I wouldn't see her for two months was asking the impossible of her. Weakened by her illness, her lack of activity, and her isolation, her life had taken a turn for the worst. How could I expect her to accept my absence?

For two days I tossed and turned in my bed and walked around town in circles, concocting every possible and imag-

inable excuse to give my mother. I constructed endless sce-
narios which could account for my two-month absence, to
no end.

On my way to her place, I ended up deciding to play
the adult-crisis-search-for-identity game, and to say that I
needed total seclusion to think about myself, that I was
bored at work, that it wasn't going well with Jenny, that I
was out of it, and that it was all getting to me! Then I imagined the discussion I was going to have with her:

"I'm your mother and I don't have anything to do with
this."

"I don't have anything against you, but I have to separate myself from you for two months. It's not such a long
time."

"It's a very long time!"

"I need it . . . for my mental stability, for my future. . . ."

I stopped at our "family eatery" for a rum raisin ice
cream, telling myself that my mother would be reassured by
the smell of this flavor on me.

She opened the door for me. She was dressed impec-
cably but with one extra accessory: a cane.

"Don't worry," she told me, "I only use it at home."

She hurried to tell me this while giving me a kiss, and
then she immediately took me by the arm and pulled me into
the living room. She gave me a Coke and took a glass of
water for herself. We drank in silence, and when she felt the
atmosphere was becoming a bit heavy, she broke the silence
with a "You know, my son," that was so serious and emo-
tionless that it chilled me to the bone.

"What is it?"

"Nothing serious or even very important, but just that Dr. Houry prescribed two weeks of thalassotherapy and two months of rest at a spa in Miami Beach."

"Two months? Isn't that a lot?"

"I know, but according to him, at my age, I've got to lower my blood pressure, take care of the problems in my joints, and get over this ongoing fatigue that I can't seem to shake. Actually, according to him, I should be there for a minimum of three months."

"If that's what he says, there's not much you can do."

"But the worst part is that I can't have any visits or phone calls. It's got to be total isolation."

"Now, that's going to be really long and hard."

"No, it's not that long and I really need it for my health. But he promised me that if you want to know how I am, you can contact him whenever you want."

I remained silent. My fate preceded me with these solutions. Everything was going in the direction of my choice, and providence obeyed me.

"So when are you leaving?"

"Dr. Houry told me that a place will be opening up in a week."

"How are you going to get there?"

"By plane. But I'll be accompanied and someone will meet me. Dr. Houry is very well known and respected there. According to him, I'll be fine. Don't worry."

IV

During the whole seclusion period I was alone with myself and my courage was failing me. Doubt would carry me away and certainty would bring me back in waves which made me seasick. I had learned enough cooking to put together a bite to eat at the end of my fasts. I had put myself on an unofficial Ramadan in order to make up for all those I hadn't observed since puberty.

My days followed a rhythm that I built around fasting, praying, Koran reading, eating, and doing a bit of housework. These were divided into segments minute by minute, prayer by prayer.

In all of these divine obligations and religious duties I had imprisoned time to manage my freedom, limit my imagination, and avoid going mad. Each act reminded me that I shouldn't forget that I was on the path of God toward martyrdom. I had to submit my entire will to God by submitting myself entirely to Him. My submission was becoming vital, necessary, and I had to cultivate it. I had to filter out my rebellion so I could trap it, I don't know where or how. I missed my mother's science. She could've helped me by modifying my genes, and making my task easier for me, making me resistant to anxieties and demons, like modified corn is resistant to all manner of pests.

I had to find another way of adopting another self.

I would have liked to be able to erase myself and then redraw me differently, but how to erase myself?

To fulfill the desire to erase myself, I had to find the space of my erasure. Would this space be my original past?

Is recapturing the past now, in an updated context, the best picture of the future? What path brought this question to me? My bastard state? My multicultural upbringing? My distress? My ignorance? I was assaulted by a series of questions and I realized that I was a pathetic philosopher.

Who will say the word which sends me to death, to make me recognize that my life is perhaps a tribute to my beliefs? Tell me and I will know!

Don't let me know this in my solitude, because it has an intelligence that Western thought will be able to encounter only in courtrooms and then it'll be too late, especially since I didn't vote for your laws. So then how can they apply to me, the victim? Liberal powers administer the anonymous liberty of the majority, but not the liberty to exist of the average person. Anyway . . .

I ran after my demons in a fog and through evanescent dawns in search of a prophecy that would have the taste of McDonald's, the emptiness of Sunday afternoons, the boredom of success, and the variety of sameness.

I would give a fortune in order to see, like in poker. But rare are those who play the game by showing their cards.

I had to exile myself by naming my country of origin, by inventing my adopted country, and then by figuring out how to make the trip. I think that I succeeded in building all that intellectually in my head. Was there in me the corresponding emotion to carry me through this adventure in body-mind-spirit-thought? That's where my doubts began.

After two months, one morning at 7:30 a.m., the intercom in my lobby buzzed. It was Athman. When I opened the door for him, he seemed radiant to me but very anxious. I felt like I was opening the door to a total stranger. He was struck by my reaction and said, "What's the matter with you? Don't you recognize me?"

"Of course I do, why?"

"You seem strange . . . it's me, Athman!"

"I know! What's going on with you?"

"Nothing. I am so excited I have butterflies in my stomach."

"What do you mean?"

"It's on! We have to meet at our training site!"

"When?"

"You, tomorrow morning, and me, at the end of the afternoon."

"You want some coffee? It's still hot."

"No thanks, I have to go."

"Do you have the address?"

"No, but tomorrow at six o'clock Jamal will be waiting for you at his place. You'll do morning prayers with him
and he'll go with you."

"And what about you?"

"I'll be there at about six p.m. for sunset prayers. This'll
be the first prayer we'll all do together."

"Who's the 'we all'?"

"The group who will do the action. OK, I've gotta run.
Don't forget to destroy all traces of your presence before leaving, and don't bring anything with you. See you tomorrow."

I closed the door behind him and I sat down at the
kitchen table, my knees giving out. For Athman this news
was a rendezvous with destiny. As for me, I was less enthu-
siastic. I was about to leave for training without knowing
what would become of me by the end. Since my father's
death I desperately struggled to find in myself this "me"
which would be capable of meeting my father at any moment, whenever I needed. I felt the physical need to see him
again so often that my body would break down completely.
I had trouble breathing, my heart missed a beat, and the tips
of my fingers would freeze. His absence panicked me. As
soon as I washed my face and drank a glass of water I would
recover from my panic. This disruption prevented me from
knowing if I too was at the rendezvous of my destiny or if I
just needed to see my father again. As the French say, "Miss-
ing a single person can make the whole world seem empty."

After finishing my morning coffee and clearing the table,
I decided to do a deep housecleaning. I scrubbed everything:

windows, doors, the floor, the chairs, everything. By noon the apartment was spotless, ready to be rented out again. I put my dirty linen, including the sheets and pillowcase on which I slept, in bags I dropped off to be washed, then I took the bus to the Hamza mosque to do the afternoon prayers near the pillar of my repentance. The mosque was almost empty. There was only the muezzin and two others praying. I had the entire space up to the *mihrab* all to myself. I was my own imam. The first "God is great" that I intoned sent me into a state of bliss. I continued my prayer in extraordinary tranquillity. My decision to go all the way took root in this state of deep calm.

While I was out I walked across the city and the idea of going to see my mother crossed my mind, with no effect. I preferred to concentrate on my solitude. This stroll turned out to be surprising; I saw things only in their details as if I were walking around wearing magnifying glasses that enlarged objects, streets, stores, signs, people. I had lost all sense of the whole to the point that I no longer knew on which street or avenue I was walking.

After buying some apples, bananas, bread, and milk, I came back home for sunset prayers. Then I made a vegetarian meal and sat down for a long reading session of the Koran, until 11:30 p.m. when I went to sleep.

At six in the morning as planned, I rang Jamal's door. One of his servants greeted me and took me to the living room. Jamal came in from the bathroom, a towel around his neck. He greeted me, tossed the towel on one of the chairs, and settled into the place designated for prayer. Having done my ritual cleansing at my place, I took off my shoes and joined Jamal. Out of respect I placed myself at his right, one step behind him. After prayers, he sat down cross-legged, his back to the wall, and asked me to sit across from him. He said to me:

"You asked me to arrange your repentance, and I did so. Every time a Muslim rejoins the ranks, I am very happy about it, and when it's thanks to me, I am proud of it. In Islam, the act of repentance is concluded by the allegiance, the *moubaya'a*. All *Jahilites* paid allegiance to the Prophet when they decided to rejoin Islam, like Abu Sufyan. Today, I'm going to have you accompanied to a place where you and others will be religiously trained to a superior level. Each of you will put his skills at the disposition of the cause in order to finalize an action which will be of major importance for all Muslims. You have to understand, I chose you, and I am responsible for you in the eyes of my fathers and in the eyes of God. This prayer that we just said together is a pact of reciprocal loyalty. Me, faithful to your repentance, and you, faithful to my guidance on the path of God. Whatever happens, you answer to me and together we answer to God. Let's say a supplication together:

"Praise be to Allah Who has made us live again after having us
die. It is to Him that the resurrection returns. Praise be to
Allah Who has given me good health in my body, has returned
my soul to me and has allowed me to invoke Him. O Allah!
Put in my heart a light, in my tongue a light, in my vision a
light, above me a light, beneath me a light, at my right a light,
at my left a light, before me a light, behind me a light, within

me a light, make of me a light. O Allah! Give me a light, put in my nerves a light, in my flesh a light, in my blood a light, in my hair a light, and in my skin a light.

"O Allah! Put a light in my tomb . . . and illuminate my bones and add in me light and give me light on light.

"*Amin,* O God of the universe."

The servant came to inform Jamal that breakfast was served. A buffet of astonishing variety was set out. The aromas were stimulating and the colors cheerful, but I was able to swallow only some coffee despite my host's repeated invitations. At 8 a.m. I left Jamal in the car of Yakoub the former servant. After ten miles or so he stopped at the parking lot of a packing company near a car in which a man was reading a local newspaper and despite the heat dressed in a red and black checked wool lumber jacket and wearing a baseball cap. Yakoub went up to him. He whispered two or three words in his ear, and then came back toward me and invited me to get in the man's car. Without saying a word I got in next to the driver and when Yakoub was at a distance, our cowboy started the car. After a few minutes, he told me, "I'm so fake as an American that I look like a real one."

"I'm just the opposite."

"What do you mean?"

"I'm so real as an American that I look like a fake one."

He burst out laughing and said, "That's what America's all about. It's one in the other. It's all and nothing."

"But it's not nothing at all."

"That's for sure. I mean, that it's as false as it is true."

"Don't you think it's a little warm to wear a wool lumber jacket?"

"Think for two minutes about the guy who decides to testify against me. He'll tell the police: 'I saw him on August tenth at 9 a.m. in a car, and he was wearing a wool lumber jacket.' Right away that sounds false because the police are not idiots. In life you've always got to cover your tracks!"

This was the only exchange we had in two and a half hours on the road. He dropped me off in the middle of a town, on the corner of a street in front of a bar, the Killarney, which was at the intersection of two streets: Mulberry and Main, and then he said to me, "We're going to do the exchange here because it's one of the few towns in America where they don't have enough funds to install surveillance cameras. So the risk is reduced as much as possible."

"Who am I supposed to wait for? And for how long?"

"A metallic maroon Chevy will pick you up in a half hour. The license plate says GO BILLS."

He repeated the plate ID to be sure I remembered, then slammed the door and left. I watched him drive away and disappear around a corner, then I wound up going into a small restaurant to get a coffee while I was waiting. A stupid little bell activated by the door made the girl behind the counter jump. She was a gorgeous, large-breasted blonde with curly hair that went on forever and a derriere emphasized by tight jeans, a real model for a trucker's calendar. In a flash, this half-dark place which stunk of mold and stale beer, with a torn, worn-out pool table, was lit up by her presence. I couldn't stop myself from walking out and saying, "Sorry, wrong place . . ."

I went up the street and came back down again taking the opposite sidewalk. A heavy humidity hung over this town which was nonexistent on any map, an aesthetic zero, and I smiled to realize how indifferent I was to the world around me. In fact, we are really linked to our environment by very few things: the pleasure of having a beer, smoking a cigarette, getting together with friends to eat the same thing and talk about the same thing. . . . The year is chopped up into holidays which all come at the same time and in the same way so that you have only one concern: how to re-celebrate even more faithfully than you did before and build up each year's little emotions, only to end up at the end of twenty years with a kitty big enough to constitute a memory. I think that life is unreal and that it takes a lot of imagination to construct its simplest reality. All these needs that promise us intoxication, all that food to whet our appetites, all those scenic trips to preserve our dreams, they all represent a colossal effort for nothing. Because no alcohol will wash away pain, no sugary-sweet candy will take away a bitter taste in the mouth, and no paradise beach will erase the nightmare, but religion can do all of this. Religion is the all-inclusive price to cover our hunger, it's the antidote to pain, it's the voyage by which dreams are fulfilled. It's the wave that brings you back and never carries you off!

When I looked right and left on the street to put my thoughts to the test, I saw that the maroon Chevy was already there. Without a word I opened the door and sat down next to the driver, a young man about thirty years old wearing Ray-Ban sunglasses and whose tan was set off by the sky blue of his T-shirt. He answered my *As-salaam alaikum* with a bright smile, and when I asked him how he could see with those sunglasses on such an unsunny day, he answered me, "I see especially with the eyes of my heart which are the eyes of faith."

I thought that from then on, I should quit asking such questions because, unlike them, I didn't have a sufficient background in my Islamic culture to find answers like the one my driver just gave me. If Islam was for me a recovery of my sense of belonging to an origin, this belonging didn't necessarily mean that I would have the instincts and culture that went with that origin.

Recovering one's meaning, is that to give meaning to oneself? Or do I rather give meaning to myself in the way that I recover it? My approach could be the opposite of the self-definition that I'm looking for. My driver, who sensed that I was lost in thought, said to me, "We're not far now. We'll be there in twenty minutes."

After a minute he turned off the highway and onto a magnificent oak-lined drive leading up to an armored gate at the end that slid open as soon as the car came to a stop. The driver said to me jokingly," The gate recognizes the car before the driver! That's America for you."

And he added, "This house belongs to the forty-third child, barely five years old, of an emir."

The gate opened onto a red brick dwelling. The house was large without being rich or luxurious. The surrounding porch was made out of a gray metallic framework held

up by ochre-colored Tuscan pillars. The driver dropped me
off at the front steps where a respectful and jovial man in
jeans, polo shirt, and Reeboks ushered me in. He led me to
the basement, and at the end of a long hallway he opened a
door to a room painted in white which had a single bed in
the corner, a large rug, and another prayer rug facing in the
direction of the Kaaba. There was a Koran on the night table
and, behind the door, a small refrigerator filled with water,
fruit, and juice. In the middle of the room there was a table
and a chair, and facing the bed there was a bathroom. It was
air conditioned and there were no windows. My escort told
me to make myself at home and to rest, and especially not
to budge until he came to get me. He added that he would
bring me my meal. He locked the door on his way out. He
came back fifteen minutes later with a tray that had a plate
with a piece of fish, some rice, and a slice of bread. He put
it down on the table and went out again. I could open my
door from the inside, but I had no key to lock it from the
outside. I ate. I washed up. I performed my ablutions. And
after my afternoon prayers I slipped into a deep sleep where
I continued my voyage.

A little before sunset prayers the escort came to get me.
While putting on my slippers, I asked him his name. He told
me, "Call me El Afghani."

"You're Afghan?"

"I might as well be."

I followed him through this house which was devoid
of furniture, where decoration was kept to a bare minimum.
He brought me into a big room covered with carpets. Three
sheikhs seated cross-legged with their backs to the wall were

waiting for me. I took off my slippers at the doorway and went toward them. I kissed all three of them on the head and I sat on my knees, heels to buttocks, facing them at a respectful distance. The main guide was apparently the one in the middle and the other two were his assistants. The one on the right said, "Oh! Raouf, from this moment on and for as long as you are in this house, you will communicate with no one, you will utter a word to no one, and you will do what you are told to do. You will leave your room only at the times indicated to you, and only to do what will be indicated to you."

He gave me a package and told me: "This is a shroud. You will wear it under your clothes and you will sleep with it on. And you will cover your head with this hood. You will show only your mouth and your eyes. You will eat alone and your food will be served you by El Afghani at the appointed time and of the quality decided by us. All these strict controls are not meant to put you in prison, may God protect us from it, but to bring you out of your prison made up of useless, harmful, and in certain cases, dangerous liberties. God said:

'ON the day when the Spirit and the Angels stand up in a row, they shall not speak to each other except he who has received permission from the Merciful and who will say what is right.' (S78, V38)

The best way to submit to God is to learn to submit to oneself. Your isolation is a return to oneself which opens doors to the fullness of your being so that it can be submitted fully to God, whatever God's will may be. You have been chosen by men, true, but these men are only the expression of the will of God Who has designated you for this immense task. May God direct our step, define the way which leads to rectitude, may He support our acts and may He accord us mercy. *Amin.* Go get dressed, and come back for the sunset prayer."

Once in my room, I opened the package which contained my shroud. It was identical to the one in which my father had been buried. I got undressed, I pushed the table aside, and I lay down nude on the floor in the middle of the room. I wanted to feel the nakedness of a corpse, the poverty of a man without a soul, the impotency of a being without life and I remembered the way that, at the age of eighteen, I had come to grips with death. At that time I had said to myself: I didn't exist before my birth and I will no longer exist after my death. Just as I didn't know I was going to exist before my birth, why should I know after my death that I existed? Because I never missed not existing before my birth, I don't see why I should miss no longer being there after my death.

I lived for fifteen years convinced of this approach. How idiotic we can be in wanting to rationalize fear. I thought of my mother. . . .

I got up, performed my ablutions, put on my shroud and got dressed. I put the table back where it was, and I began reading the Koran, waiting for El Afghani to come to get me.

At sunset prayers all five of us in the action group, hooded, came together in the big room. El Afghani and another, El Yemeni, were our intermediaries for the general organization, stage managers, as it were.

The assistant who spoke to me at my arrival began:

"Before getting up for prayer, all five of you are going to take the oath of your submission to God, of your faith in Islam, and of your honor as a Muslim. For that, I let the Master Guide speak."

The guide looked us in the eye one by one, then asked each of us to hold the Koran in our right hand and to repeat after him:

"In the name of God the All-Merciful. I swear in the name of God:

'SAY: God is He, the Unique.
God. The Supreme refuge.
He begot none nor was He begotten.
None could be His equal or like.' (S112)

'BY God, we shall not sell our testament at any price, not even to a near relative, nor shall we conceal the testimony of God, for then we should surely be amongst criminals.' (S5, V106)

'PRAISE be to God, Lord and Master of all worlds. The Merciful in essence and in excellence. Master of the Day of Judgment. It is You whom we adore! And it is from You that we implore aid. Guide us on the straight path. The path of those whom You have touched with Your Grace, and not of those who have incurred Your Wrath, nor of those who have gone astray.' (S1)

"*Amin*, O God of the universe."

❊   ❊   ❊

After the prayer, the guide spoke:

"Dear Martyrs,

"From my first word to you today until my last on the day that you leave, I'm going to distill for you the sense of the words, the contours of the faith. I'm going to nourish your spirit on the immensity of God's space and the immensity of His Mercy, but also on the immensity of His Punishment.

"God requires submission and He does the rest! Your entire will must be in the exercise of your submission to God, Who will take charge of your request, and of your soul, as well as your body. This means your life in the Hereafter.

"Submitting oneself to God is not submitting oneself to a superior.

"Submitting oneself to God is not submitting oneself to the devil.

"Submitting oneself to God is not submitting oneself to one's desires.

"All these submissions are debasing and humiliating. They lend to man neither dignity, nor honor, nor grandeur. The one and only submission which reconstitutes, which revitalizes, which revalorizes being is the submission to God. Submitting oneself to God is to invest oneself totally in the Magnificence of God. It is to reverse the value scale because we are in the grandeur of the infinite.

"Submitting oneself to human desires is to debase oneself.

"Submitting oneself to God is to be elevated.

"How to be glorified by submitting oneself? It's a path that we're going to take together, and for that, I will begin by speaking to you of dream and of death in Islam. Why dream and death? What is the relationship between the two? According to the Judeo-Christians, death is dreamt by no one and no one dreams of dying. This, dear faithful, is their point of view. In our religion the relationship between dream and death is totally different. It is said in the Sacred Book:

> 'ALLAH takes away from human beings their souls at the moment of their death as well as from those who do not die during their sleep. He holds on to the soul of those whose death He has decreed and He releases the others for an appointed term fixed in advance. In this, there are signs for those that reflect.' (S39, V42)

"This means that when we are sleeping, our soul leaves our body and travels through space and time. It sees what is invisible to us, it encounters people we've never met or who are already dead, it passes through distances and travels to places we've never been. That is dream. When the sleeper is a true Believer, God authorizes his soul to meet a part of Allah's truth and knowledge in the dream world. When this soul comes back to its body, it transmits back to the sleeper this truth and knowledge that God let him glimpse. This is called: the real dream, the just dream, or the truthful dream.

"The soul can also travel freely depending on the night and quality of the sleep, and on the state of the soul of the sleeper, but what it learns, what it glimpses is false. This voyage in the false is the normal, ordinary dream. It's this one that interests the psychoanalysts, for psychoanalysis is only the art of reading perversion in false dreams and of thus maintaining souls on the path of perdition. For psychoanalysis doesn't correct perversion, it makes the patient admit it. It's the art of stabilizing, of maintaining the diabolical in the human being!

"In Islam death is a great voyage of the soul, and a dream is the little voyage of the soul. One can say that sleep is a little death and death, a big dream.

"In the sleep state, the soul is not totally separated from the body, because one can be awakened at any time, contrary to what happens during death, which is an exile of the soul into another world. . . . In this case the body is forever fixed where its soul left it, whereas it meets the *barzakh* or the *isthmus* which is the go-between and which delineates the space between death and resurrection for the last judgment. God says:

> 'WHEN death comes to one of them [a heathen] he says: Lord! Let me be sent back to Earth. Perhaps then might I accomplish good works amongst the things I left behind! No! These are futile words he uttered; a *barzakh* lies behind them till the Day they will be resurrected.' (S23, V99–100)

"The *isthmus* is the space where human will is of no help, where man cannot master events and where distance, time, and the rest don't have the same dimension.

"Thus, according to Islam, dream and death are linked to the same space: the *barzakh*. About this, the Prophet teaches us: *'By God your death will assuredly be akin to your sleep, and your resurrection will be akin to your waking.'*

"So we see that dreams are only one step on the path to death. It's as if God in His generosity has gotten us used to our death, little by little every night.

"Thus the accomplishment of dream is death. This is why a consistent Muslim, sure of his faith, can only dream of death. God tells us:

'DARE wish for death if you are sincere.' (S2, V94)

"But what is death? Throughout the Holy Book there are more than eighty verses that speak of death. Eighty verses not to explain to us what death is, for death is unexplainable because it's divine will. God gives and takes away life to and from whom He wishes, where He wishes, and when He wishes. It is in this sense that we are His subjects. Our existence and our life depend strictly on God and on God alone. But then why are there eighty verses to talk about it? From sura 2 to sura 84 God mentions death at different times, in different contexts:

'GOD said to Jesus: I will have you suffer death and I will lift you up to Me, I will purify you and I will deliver you from the unbelievers. I will put those who have followed you above the heathens until the day of resurrection, when you will all come back to Me and I will pass judgment on the differences among you. (S3, V55)

'Remember the elders of the Children of Israel after the death of Moses when they told one of their Prophets: "Raise up for us a king and we shall fight on the path of God." (S2, V246)

'Were you witnesses when death came upon Jacob, when he asked his sons: "What will you worship after me?" They answered, "We will worship your God, the God of your fathers, Abraham, Ishmael, and Isaac. God, the only One, for whom we will be Muslims."' (S2, V133)

"If the Koran speaks so much about death, it's because our relationship with God is established through death. It is reported that the Sheikh Abu al-Darda said: 'I love death, for I passionately want to meet my Lord.'

"It is reported that just before his death the great servant of God Hudhayfa said, 'I love death, and it comes exactly at the time I need it. He who regrets it will not succeed.'

"God has given us our life in the Here and Now solely to be able to choose our second life, our real life, the one He will give us after death. The choice is made based on the relationship you will establish with death in accordance with your faith. Thus, God has power over our life and our death. Our only power is to live a life that deserves a death that God will be able to reward by giving us another, better life. It all happens as if God, in His generosity, had given us this life Here and Now which can be unsatisfactory, unlucky, problem ridden, rich or poor, so we may choose the second one. No one is responsible in the first life for birth, fortune, or success. . . . But each of us is responsible for the choices that determine our second life. If our first life is imposed upon us, the second is our own choice.

"If you are confident of your faith, if you are at peace with your actions, if you are sure of what is in your hearts, at this moment you will not even need 'to dare desire death.' It will become a natural desire, an aspiration guided by your faith, and the decision in the choice of the hour, day, or month of the year is in God's hands. It is said:

> 'AND so comes the intoxication of death at the same time as truth, which is what you always tried to avert.' (S50, V19)

"What does God mean by 'the intoxication of death'? It's this instant that can be as uplifting as it is painful; it's the moment when life and death cross, the moment when death defies life and when the one dying resists. During these fleeting instants he sees his future place either in Paradise or in hell. Thus, he has a true idea of the truth of the Scriptures for one can live as a heathen, but one never leaves this world uninformed of the truth. And the dying one will know what was or what wasn't his conviction. That's why in the Koran death is also called *yaqin*, certainty or conviction:

> 'WORSHIP God until certainty comes to you. [El-Yaqin "death"].' (S15, V99)

"Why are death and certainty linked? Each of these two words carries in it the dimension of the other. To be convinced is to be so until death because we labor our entire life in order to affirm our certainty and because it's at the moment of death that our certainty recognizes us. So then, it's our convictions throughout our life which lead us toward the choice of our death. That's why choice isn't often made about 'dying' or 'not dying,' but about 'being convinced of one's faith' or 'not being convinced of one's faith.' Death remains a decision of God. If God decides that you should stay alive, you will stay alive no matter what happens. How many examples do we have where death was certain, but where God decided the opposite? Because life and death are one and the same thing: God's decision and nothing else. If you are alive, it's God's decision. If you die tomorrow, it's God's decision. So what's the difference? And yet, there is at least one difference. In life, you earn what the ordinary mortal earns: a limited, expendable salary that can be used up. In death, you earn what a living person earns for eternity: an unexpendable salary, unlimited and unending. That's the real difference between life and death. God tells us:

> 'SUCH is the reward for your earthly acts, for truly
> God is not unjust to His servants.' (S3, V182)

"It is reported that the great believer Ali ibn Sahl implored God in a sad voice before going to sleep: 'Ah, Lord! For how long will You condemn me to remain prisoner in the Here and Now? Fulfill in me Your beautiful promise by taking me to meet You in the Hereafter, because You know that I am eager for it and that the waiting has lasted too long.'

"Allah, Allah, my Lord! O Allah! We put You in their throats and we take refuge at Your side from their wrongdoings. O Allah! You are my support and my defender, it's through You that I champion Your cause, and it is for You that I do battle.

"Peace be with you."

At the end of the speech, the assistant, a jurist, enjoined each of us to return to our rooms, where dinner awaited us, before meeting again for the evening prayers, the *Al-Isha*. Alone with my lentil soup and dessert of milk and rice cake, I told myself that this recognition of my oath by men of God and by God was bringing me great relief. I was past the point of having to struggle against pain; I was now able to prevent it from getting to me. I had succeeded in turning things around. I was no longer in a defensive position; I was on the offensive, and a step ahead. It was no contest, a battle with no risk of losing but with the certainty of winning. This lentil soup was delicious!

I was putting the hood back on when El Afghani knocked on my door.

After the *Al-Isha* prayer, the second assistant, a neurologist and psychiatrist, spoke:

"After 'In the name of God the Merciful,' in Islam, no religious act is possible without purification as described by the precepts. Our Prophet tells us, 'Purity is half of faith.' And God tells us in the Koran:

'ALLAH loves those who repent and those who purify themselves.' (S2, V222)

"The water which you use to purify yourselves must itself be pure and placed in a purified receptacle. Once washed, you will proceed to the act of purification by the ablutions in order to prepare for prayer, that is, to acknowledge your submission to God through genuflection and the *khouchou*. All this purification, which has no other meaning than to wash the body and to purify the spirit, would be valid and sufficient if we were living in a Muslim country and if we had been raised exclusively according to the laws of Islam and according to the Muslim traditions which respect the holy Book. However, it happens that Raouf was born in the United States, Athman was educated in France, Safar, the army pilot, and Omar, the army officer, were trained in the United States. Your knowledge is unquestionable. The duty of every Muslim is to expand his knowledge, for all knowledge is a gift of God. Those who say that they graduated from Harvard or from such and such a school have really graduated only from the university of God.

"This is obvious, but not so simple, because if all these heathens, all these unbelievers, all these Jews were to work or think under Muslim authority like in Andalusia, all this knowledge would be Muslim thanks to Muslim authority. But today the heathens have the power. They've wrapped God's gift of knowledge in a cultural package with the result that every Muslim, in order to acquire this knowledge, has to conform to their image and lose his soul. That's quite a price to pay for education. That's too much to pay for our modernity, our material comfort, and interaction with the heathen. They've fixed it so that by providing education they undermine the solid ground of our native cultures, and that's intolerable.

"Granted, dear martyrs, you will be able to purify your-selves for prayer! But the action that you must undertake is so demanding, as much physically, morally, and mentally as spiritually and intellectually, that we must fear that your other 'self' might still contain inhibitions which are more those of an average American than of a proud Muslim. For you must know that inhibitions are the result of a cultural and spiri-tual heritage. You who were born on God's holy soil and have been educated in America should know that this is a land God didn't deem worthy of discovery, a land which was discov-ered by accident, that is, by a lost soul who got lost.

"Thus America was born out of perdition. That's why they love to get lost. It's their only way of finding themselves. The best way to confuse the lost ones is to act more lost than they are. It's for these reasons that your action must be impossible in the eyes of men, but honorable when facing God and manageable for you. Meeting these three require-ments in your action is the proof of Islam's superiority.

"Now let's come back to the inhibitions which risk slowing you down, preventing you from going all the way. How could they trigger unpredictable behavior which could endanger the group and the action? To give you an example: you're at an airport, you're walking down a concourse look-ing for your departure gate. The police approach you for a random search. One of you will be afraid, but will hold up under the pressure. But fear is a recognizable signal to the police, and it attracts investigations and questioning. That is to be avoided.

"There will be one of you who will replace fear by an outburst: 'What's going on here? Who do you think I am?' This is also to be avoided.

"I'll stop with these two examples to say that your re-action in front of the police should be as normal as possible. The normal reaction at this time is to accept the authority of the police to which they are entitled. For the police, the suspect is the first one to question authority. That's precisely the problem! Who among you doesn't have a problem with authority? Despite the pressures you'll feel, you should be psychologically prepared to fully comply in every way with all of the authorities. Because winning, in many cases, means not speaking up in opposition, but remaining silent and submissive.

"In order to agree on the scope of the preparation sched-ule for the action, you have essentially to purify your mind and body in order to be recognizable as a Muslim by the God of the Muslims. Your life, whether you feel it or not, belongs to their culture more than to ours. You will have to change your mind set and your mental state. It is said in the Koran:

'GOD does not change the state of a people if the individuals do not change what is within them.'
(S13, V11)

"An unfortunate history has made the scales tip on the side of Western culture. You have the hearts and souls of Muslims, but intellectually and culturally you are Western-ers. You are examples of interbreeding which by definition implies a loss of spiritual purity. You carry within you the doubts, certainties, desires, and longings of others. Even though you don't take them into account, they are strapped to you like bombs nonetheless. They weaken and undermine you, they don't appear at peaceful times, but rise up in times of stress. In order to blow them up, you first have to defuse yourself. That's what this preparation schedule is all about. It's also our duty to purify future Martyrs from history's vicissitudes, from their painful pasts, in order to return them to God, purified from the failures of the *Ummah Islamiyya* and worthy of His Mercy.

"In this spirit, you are going to rest for the next five days to come. What does 'rest' mean? It means getting into a natural rhythm, that is, not staying up late, waking up at the same time every day, eating at appointed times. You will have at your disposal a gym and at specific times each of you will be able to take a walk outside with El Afghani or El Yemeni. By following this schedule, you're going to regain your physical strength, your mental balance, and your psychic energy. Then I will see each one of you to assess your state. Now I will let our guide speak. . . .

"During these five days you will read half of the Koran and we will meet only for sunset prayers which will not be followed by a sermon. May God guide and protect you."

During these five days I felt my body cleanse itself almost hour by hour. Freed of everything and focused solely on the Koran reading, I discovered the immensity of it and of everything that God has thought of for us. I would read out loud to make the words resonate in my body, to feel the holy word physically.

If God created the world in six days, these five days re-created the world for me. They re-created me for another world. I was no longer the same, and in my eyes, the world was no longer the same either. That was the beginning of rebirth. I was another person going in another way toward another world. I needed these five days of silence to listen, hear, and understand that one makes no choice in this world without its being decided by God who guides us to the choice. If not, how can I explain my presence here? Either God exists, or I am mad. My certainty is that God exists and that I'm mad for Him. Yes, I'm mad for God. Is that not the supreme wisdom, the wisdom of the weak man who submits to the immensity of God with boundless reason? We loved our parents. How can we not love our Creator?

God, I submit myself to You with the fervor of one who submits, capable of reinventing his submission every day so as to submit in a greater way each day. I adore my submission to You, God!

El Afghani brought me my breakfast. He said to me,

"According to the schedule, work meetings were planned to begin today. But the Master Guide has postponed the schedule for three days."

"And you have no idea of the reason for this postponement?"

"My brother, I'm not here to have ideas. Have a good breakfast."

These three days were no longer symbolic. They were days of waiting and that broke my momentum toward the deepening of the essential. Each day had twenty-four hours in it, each hour, sixty minutes, and each minute, sixty seconds.

We were no longer in the "what's happening inside us?" mode, but in the "what's happening outside of us?" mode. Three days? Why? And "why" is a heathen's question.

We now had to make these three days flow more continuously into the five previous ones by putting our patience back to work. If, at the end of three days, they told us again, "in twenty days," that would extend the wait for a soul which had psychologically integrated eternity in all its mental, spiritual, intellectual, and temporal facets. Waiting shouldn't have an effect on us any longer. We couldn't be waiting for God. We were with Him. The clock regulated our work schedule and daily routine, but it was of no use to great lovers and determined ones. We are already there! Up to you to choose the day and the hour; God will decide our fate for there is only His hour; all other watches tick away uselessly.

El Afghani opened the door and said, "Tonight, we'll have the sermon after prayers. You'll be eating a bit later."

During prayers the Master Guide read from the Koran longer than usual. He seemed exhilarated. As we sat down after the prayers, he was beaming and announced in a tone of satisfaction,

"My dear Martyrs, brothers in faith, today is a great day. We have been waiting for over three months for the *fatwa* that was to decree your action as an act of *jihad* and make you Martyrs of Islam. This *fatwa* reached us yesterday and makes martyrs of you. This is why our work has been delayed for three days now. This *fatwa* has come down to us from the High Council of the *Ulama* as recognized by our community. It states in effect: 'in the case of aggression taken by heathens against an Islamic country, the *jihad* becomes a sacred duty for all Muslims. Those nearest must take action first and so on down the line until all Muslims of the earth have joined forces on the battlefield.'

"So you see, my brothers, there is the opinion of our most revered *Ulama* who beg us to act, who summon us to act, not in the name of some insignificant organization but in the name of God, in the name of all Muslims. Let us give thanks to God for having enlightened us to our destiny and for having opened to us the path of the *jihad*. As our Prophet tells us: *'Submission is the building, Prayer its pillar, and Holy War the crowning glory of its dome.'*

"Thanks to God for having given us the opportunity to die as martyrs. Thanks to God for having chosen us among Muslims to become His faithful soldiers. Thanks to God for having placed us on the front line in this battle for Islam, for justice, for the Koran, for God. Thanks for having facilitated our task, for having given wisdom to our *Ulama* so that they could decree in these times of darkness the holy *jihad* which will light the way for our future. God tells us,

> 'FIGHT for the cause of God. You have to assume responsibility only for your own life. Rouse the Believers to fight: perhaps God will put an end to the heathen's aggression. God has greater might and His punishment is more severe.' (S4, V84)

"My brothers in religion and dear Martyrs, blessed be he who, like you, has been chosen by God. A Muslim who dies in peace is happy, but one who dies in battle is happier still. Khalid ibn al-Walid, the commanding chief of the army of the Prophet, proclaimed on his death bed, 'Though I participated in many battles, in many wars, never was I struck by an arrow or a saber. Today I am nearing death in my bed like a camel. May God curse the cowards who never touched me in battle! And may they never find a moment's rest.'

"In speaking of the martyr, the Prophet said: *'The Martyr receives six rewards from Allah: He pardons him as soon as his blood is shed and He leads him to his place in Paradise. He spares him the punishment of the tomb, He protects him against the "great terror," He places on his head a crown of dignity in which a single ruby has greater value than the world and all within it, He marries him to seventy-two dark-eyed houris and He permits him to intercede on behalf of seventy of his family members.'*

"He also said: *'When one of your brothers is killed 'in battle,' Allah places his soul among the green birds that hover over the river of Paradise where it will eat of its fruit and take shelter within golden lamps in the shadow of the Throne. When his soul has enjoyed the sweetness of this food and drink, and reveled in the splendid welcome, it will say: 'If only my brothers of Islam knew what Allah has done with me, they would never abandon the jihad, nor speak instead of secular war.'*

"And finally God said,

'Do not consider those who were killed in the cause of God as dead. On the contrary they are alive and near their Lord, abounding in His gifts.' (S3, V169)

"What grandeur in this simplicity, what beauty in this purity to tell us of the superior things which ask man to lift himself up through his intellect and his perceptiveness, and to reach understanding based on childlike innocence and genuine naïveté.

'Do not think of them as dead, but rather as alive.'
(S3, V169)

"The mind shaped by Western thinking will say that this is unthinkable: you're either dead or alive, and there is no such thing as the living dead. They are right because they do not have our faith, and our faith tells us, dictates to us, and teaches us that they are in the wrong. Everything that they think they've invented, such as science and knowledge, was invented by God. To use this knowledge and intellect with faith in God is what God determined. But if this knowledge is used to challenge and question God, it is the greatest of sins. One must never use the gifts of God against God. You might be the greatest scientist in the world, but you must still allow your most deep-rooted innocence, purity, *tahara*, to remain ever attentive to His word. It is by being the most accomplished scientist in the Here and Now and the most innocent in your faith that you will conquer the most powerful, because you will know their secrets and their thoughts, while they will never be able to comprehend the depth of your purity. Your purity is visible neither to their eyes, nor to X-rays, nor to the police. It cannot even be detected by their satellites. You are just ordinary men among them. You know, and they do not. You know that he who 'dies on the path of God' does not die and that there is no death for Martyrs, for they pass instantaneously from life in the Here and Now to life in the Hereafter. They know neither suffering nor death. Regardless of how the Martyr dies, his soul remains intact and will enter into God's presence with his body intact.

"Such are the teachings of God for those who decided to take up arms for Him. There are those who set off for war on God's path and who may or may not die; their destiny is in the hands of the Lord. But can those who engage in operations where death is certain be accused of committing suicide? Can they be accused of committing suicide? Can one commit suicide in the name of God? What then is suicide? Suicide is to give oneself over to death in a state of despair. How can one have faith in God and be in despair? That is inconceivable, impossible. That is why suicide has nothing to do with Islam. Whoever chooses suicide will go directly to hell, because, by definition, that person has no faith. Committing suicide for God amounts to saying that one gives himself to death out of hopelessness in the face of God. This would mean being an unbeliever to the point of despair, and that would only be the suicide of a desperate unbeliever.

"Not so, my brothers!

"To die as a Martyr on the path of God is to move out of the shadows into the light; to move away from a small insignificant life to a great life; to take leave of unhappiness in the Here and Now and delight in the joys of the Hereafter; to leave the dwelling of suffering for the garden of goodness. It is to be counted no longer among mortals, but to join the ranks of the immortals. Our Prophet tells us, *'Whosoever shall die, shall live on in his own resurrection.'*

"To die as a Martyr is the most beautiful life possible. Christians will never be able to understand the parables and symbols which are the reality of our faith and beliefs. In all of their churches, or above their beds and even around their necks, they hang a dying Christ on the cross as their sole Martyr. There is and there will always be only one Martyr for them: Jesus. Christians make much of Jesus' sacrifice, but they themselves do not follow his example, while in Islam every Muslim is a potential Martyr on the path toward God. We are all Jesuses, Solomons, Davids for the glory of God. We follow the lead of all of the Prophets, both theirs and ours, in seeking to defend our faith and safeguard the salvation of our souls.

"To die for God is not painful, useless, or dehumanizing for the faithful. Death is the transcendence of faith. If death is, as the heathens claim, a suffering, a hell, how could God force His faithful to undergo the hell of death before they enter into Paradise? If to die is first to suffer, then where is the serenity of the angels who enter the tomb to question the deceased about his actions? How can a man suffering in hell be questioned? Death marks the separation of the soul from the body. A body without a soul suffers no longer, and a soul without a body awaits judgment in the face of God. Only He decides on his hell or his Paradise.

"The imam Ibn al-Qayyim said: 'Be aware that the teachings of our ancestors of the *Ummah al-Salaf* are unanimous in claiming that death occurs either in sorrow, or in joy, or in pain, which applies to the soul as well as to the body. Once the soul leaves the body, it undergoes punishment or is treated to eternal happiness. Together, body and soul experience the same pain or the same bliss.' For that reason, regardless of what physical shock your body encounters at the moment of the explosion, you yourself will feel no pain because your soul is at peace. God in His generosity says:

> 'GOD will impose on no soul a burden greater than it can bear. Whatever it will have done will be invoked for or against it. Lord, punish us not for mistakes committed due to forgetfulness or by mistake. Lord, do not impose on us a burden greater than that which You placed on those who lived before us. Lord, do not charge us with what we cannot bear. Take away our sins, forgive us for them, have pity on us. You are our Lord. Give us victory over the unbelievers.' (S2, V286)

"May peace be with you."

The assistant who was the neurologist and psychiatrist then spoke to us: "Tomorrow morning, we'll run a blood test on each of you before you've eaten anything to verify your state of health. Before prescribing anything, I'll have a confidential interview with each of you. On that note, I'll just say good night."

It was my first night as a potential Martyr. For which operation? Toward what objective? To what end? I still had no idea.

When I thought about my father, I was convinced of my approach, and that I was doing the right thing. When I thought about my mother, I was doubtful and very much uncomfortable. I always felt I was doing what I was doing *for* one of them and *against* the other. At least if there were

two children in the family, one would be for the father and
the other for the mother. What was I guilty of with regard to
my parents?

By accepting to be a Martyr, I was convinced of sav-
ing my father's soul as well as my mother's because they, in
wishing to save my life, would condemn my soul as well as
theirs to hell.

I swallowed the immensity of the night in little gulps,
in order to get my fill of existence and accept the idea of a
purposeful death, an arranged death.

I rolled out my fear like dough on the marble of my
heavenly tomb. There where I was supposed to be rereading my childhood, I was rereading the Koran. It was peace,
argument, and reason. Little by little I slipped into the kingdom of the peaceful and convinced souls. Like a real desert
traveler for whom the route is always there despite the sand
giving way under his feet, with a scrap of bread for subsis-
tence and a star as my guide.

The Here and Now has taken over our vision; it has
made us dream of spaces with inaccessible horizons. But our
fractures compounded with wounds will be sufficiently serious to give us the right to break away for the Hereafter.

When I was awakened for the sunrise prayers, I felt that I
had slept very little but I wasn't nervous.

After the ablutions and the group prayer in the sermon
hall, each of us retired to his room to read the passages from
the Koran that were assigned us.

Tarik, the resident doctor, arrived at about nine o'clock
in a room on the main floor, which was set up as an infir-
mary. We were each called in for a blood draw. As Tarik

untied the rubber tourniquet from my arm, he asked, "Were you born in the United States?"

"Yes, I was born in Baltimore."

"So you're an American by birth. How do you feel about becoming a Martyr?"

"It's true I'm an American, but my God isn't American."

"And between the two, do you choose God over America?"

"America is against my God. The proof? If one day as an American, I get to be a candidate for the presidency of the United States, do you think that they'd accept me taking the oath of office on the Koran instead of the Bible? They'd have to change the Constitution. So, in essence America is against my God."

"But it's the same thing in our countries."

"In the meantime America is the model for our countries. When the model is unjust, it must be broken. Only after that will we be able to improve the situation in our home countries."

"What's the underlying reason that motivates you to participate in this action?"

"My father's death took me by surprise just when we were on the verge of becoming friends, I mean, speaking to each other on the same level, laughing at the same things; basically, just at the time when I was beginning to relate to my father as a man. He died in a work accident and I never accepted or understood the reasons for his death. Without even knowing it, this extra weight on my soul made me want to get beyond this pain. The worst was that when I went to the cemetery with my mother, I had nothing inside of me that, spiritually speaking, helped me to meet my father somewhere in my mind. In front of his tomb, I was really, spiritually and objectively speaking, only in front of a stone, and visiting my father seemed ridiculous to me, although my father was never ridiculous to me. . . ."

I don't know why but I broke out sobbing. Tarik calmly had me move over. He gave me a tissue and told me gently to continue. . . .

"Athman and Jamal helped me and guided me toward repentence. Neither of them knew my story. At the time of my father's death I felt that my life took a turn for the worse. But after my repentance, I was convinced that my life had taken a turn for the better. I'm no longer the same person as before my father died, and I'm no longer the same person after, either. I'm a different person. . . ."

"So what's your most important reason for participating in the action?"

"To be with my father again. I think that he would not have accepted me dying young, but meeting the dead through death is a Western point of view which does not take into account the quality of the death. In Islam, the reason for the death affects the quality of the death. I especially want to die as a Martyr to redeem my father's sins in the eyes of God, the Greatest and most Merciful, and bring him to my side in Paradise. My father suffered as a result of those years of exile. The winters were rough and he didn't get a vacation in the summer and, in order to hold on, he drank and he must have committed all kinds of sins. I even think he was a member of the Omar Brotherhood, or the Freemasons, I don't know. On the other hand, his death was due to a work-related accident, but they never wanted to admit it. It's not because they refused to pay, because the death compensation wouldn't have set them back all that much. But rather it was as if they just didn't want to admit that accidents happen at their work place and that my father killed himself working for them. It's the kind of common, everyday injustice that I want to make them pay for. That's why this trip means so much to me. It's really my ascension toward my father so that our love can be re-born in Paradise."

"It's almost Christian, but it's still divine! May God keep you under His veil and under His mercy. May He grant you what you are looking for and may peace be with you. You can go rest now in your room."

He asked El Afghani to take me back and to bring in Athman.

I lay down on the bed, amazed at the coherence of my speech in front of Tarik. I was proud of myself. I was almost ecstatic in discovering that I could maintain clear thinking about my life and express it philosophically. Up until now I was moving forward in this adventure without really know-ing what my part was in the conflicts and risks. Now I knew. I had never really felt the fact of knowing as clearly as I did now. These few words I had said to Tarik had connected all the synapses in my cortex and I felt that I was in the right. But being in the right doesn't mean anything. I had my own truth that I would die for, since living this truth meant pass-ing through death. I had finally made it. . . . Thank God.

Our first work session began in the afternoon after midday prayers in the workroom. In the left wing of the house, a hallway opened on two rooms facing each other, equipped with desks and computers and the first also serving as a li-brary. In effect, the house was split in two with one side for sleep and religion and the other for work and cooking. In the middle of the hall on a plaque set into the floor separating the two sides of the house was written: "What is decided here is achieved here," and the words "achieved here" and "decided here" were underlined with two opposite arrows which pointed to the two spaces separated by the plaque. And above this sentence, there was an arrow pointing upward to the inscription "For God."

The work meeting was opened by the assistant who was a jurist and in charge of giving a presentation on the politics of the situation.

"The United States and the Western world declare their loyalties to Greco-Roman antiquity, to the pharaohs, but not to the Arab-Islamic civilizations. Their civilization is termed Judeo-Christian, their modernity western, denying the contribution of the other half of the world. They forget that America was itself discovered thanks to progress made by Arabs in navigation. And if an Arab had been at the helm, he would have discovered America knowing it was America and not the Indies. This is proof from the start that Europeans were wrong about America.

"Moreover, we helped the Western world stop the evolution of materialist ideas and communism in the Arab and Muslim world. We also had quite a bit to do with the fall of the Berlin Wall. Today, if we look at the map of wars in the world, we will see that the targets are Islam and Muslims.

"On the one hand, we have the Gulf countries which pay the Americans for their security, autonomy, and comfort in petrodollars, and on the other hand, we have the rest of the Muslims in the world who pay with their lives for the glory of the West and the Jews, whether it's in the Middle East, in Sudan, in Iraq, or in the rest of Asia. All Muslims are seen as plague-stricken, inherently useless and dangerous. We are good for only one thing: to justify their wars to increase their power. The Americans profit from everything: decolonization came about so they could take over the colonies; the defeat of Nazism is their victory; the fall of the Berlin Wall is their victory too. That's how the powerful become even more powerful. But we will never be able to defeat this superpower by staying on the playing field of its logic. We won't make the same mistakes as Hitler and the Russians. Hitler fought them with the same tools. With this kind of conflict, it's simply a question of being stronger. The Soviet Bloc ran itself out of breath economically, in a frantic arms race.

"According to this kind of logic, the West is unbeatable. So where is its weak point?

"Western power does have its weak points. One of these weak points is having developed this power out of the fear of death. They've multiplied life's pleasures out of fear of not having lived enough before death. They dared to expand their power in order to live a Paradise before their death and to make their Here and Now a Paradise-like Hereafter determined by their power. Our Prophet tells us: *"The life of Here and Now is the prison of the believer and the Paradise of the unbeliever."* They show a great disregard for God, for only God decides who amongst us deserves Paradise and He makes the decision beyond our death. Their weak point is this fear of death which makes them forget their humility in front of God. The only answer is to risk death for our God and to humiliate them in order to reestablish honor, not only that of Islam, but God's honor in the heart of all Muslims. We have to strike them in a way they can't imagine, right where they least expect it, and with a strength they can't fathom.

"Within our hearts and through our faith this is our vision of things. That's what will unite you in our action. You are all looking toward the same light. We will tell them that as for us, we are not afraid of death because our death is another life in the hands of God. Our power is in our duty to accept death for the Hereafter, theirs is in their desire to live in the Here and Now. They don't want us to live like them, although they prove to us that they're capable of dying like us. Those are the two halves of the equation. Your success consists in fulfilling the requirements for the ordeal in your life Here and Now, in order to entitle you to this beautiful death which will guarantee your Hereafter in the mercy of God.

"It's up to us to point out to them their impotence despite their power, proving to them that we dominate over their technological efficiency and that we can turn it against them, under their own noses, in their own country. Then perhaps they will quit taking us for idiots capable of nothing and incapable of everything.

"If those in the West were capable of understanding the world, they would have a more sympathetic relationship with it. If they were capable of speaking to the world, we would have heard them. They waged war in the name of peace, and in the name of peace they only know how to make war again. Where is their understanding and where is their communication with others?

"That is, my dear brothers, what I wanted to say to you before you begin your work. I wish you total success and now I'll let Fouad speak."

"The objective for the five of us is to take possession of a civilian airplane of the Boeing type, the model of which is yet to be defined. The action will be crashing it into an established target. We'll learn of our specific target later on. For the moment, it's the feasibility that we'll be studying. The feasibility involves five major components:

1. Purchase of the tickets: this means the name under which we have to buy them, at which agency, and what each of our seating assignments has to be.
2. Going through all the airport security: cameras, electronic gates, police, etc. This especially concerns what kind of weapon we have to carry.
3. Techniques of subduing the passengers.
4. Taking control of the flight deck: how to put the plane on course for the target, which brings up the problem of the speed of maneuvers to evade defense missiles.
5. We will be with God!

"We have two weeks of work to carry out these preparations. Athman and Raouf will be responsible for plotting out and analyzing the flight parameters with the collaboration of Safar, who will be at the airplane's flight controls.

"Omar is the specialist in riot control, a martial arts and combat sports expert. He will be your instructor between sunrise prayers and breakfast. The exercises will begin under his command. Breakfast will be between eight and eight-thirty, and from eight-thirty to twelve-thirty will be theoretical work in your groups, with each group in its own room. After afternoon prayers you'll all regroup to develop the ideas of each group and to plan for the next day's work.

"Two weeks can be both long or short depending on how we function. Don't forget one thing: how we function in this work will determine how the operation as a whole will be carried out. Are we a winning group or not? That's what we'll try to build in the course of these two weeks. Are there any questions?"

I then asked, "Do we know the date of the operation?"

"The target and the date will be communicated to us at the designated time. What's sure is that the date will be set at two weeks or Hereafter."

Under the hoods, laughter could be heard. Athman then took over and said, "We would have to know very soon at least what model of plane to hijack."

"Your calculations will determine that."

"Are the morning exercises individual or collective training sessions to coordinate us on passenger control?"

"For that, I'll let Commander Omar answer." Omar got up and said,

"In the morning you'll have physical training. During the afternoon sessions we'll see how to proceed depending on each of your abilities. This operation must be entirely collaborative, and if it isn't, we won't succeed. But we'll be talking much more about this."

Fouad thanked Omar and asked again if there were any other questions. There being none, the meeting was ended. El Afghani came up to me and said, "I'm taking you back to your room. Dr. Atik, the psychiatrist, will be coming to see you."

While waiting for Atik I tried to jog my memory about technical information I had learned at Boeing. I never would have believed that the six months of training I had was going to be so instrumental in my life.

El Afghani knocked at the door. Atik was with him. He asked me to sit down in front of him and said a few words which put me at ease. I barely heard him ask me to recount the day in my life when I had been the most frightened, before slipping under . . . as if I had been anesthetized.

The day of my greatest apprehension and fear was the day I had to go to the funeral home with my mother. I had put off as long as possible the moment of seeing my father's dead body, but after that morning there would never be another chance. I couldn't put it off any longer. I couldn't get out of it. I had to see him.

My mother was afraid of my reaction. That's why we arrived earlier, before everyone else. He was in a green satin-lined casket, dressed in a black suit with a white shirt and a tie. My mother had even put his glasses on him so he wouldn't look too different. I don't know if it was the smell of the flowers or of the embalming fluid, I don't know where the smell came from that suddenly made me sick. I had just enough time to put my hand over my mouth so as not to splatter my morning coffee all over my father. My mother took a handkerchief from her purse and gave it to me. She led me to the restroom and told me to go wash my face. Then she took some toilet paper to clean up the floor next to the casket.

With my head in the sink under the cold water, I could hear my father's lute as he had me practice the scales. I dunked my head all the way into the sink. My mother came back into the restroom and pulled my head out of the water. I was so sick that I couldn't feel a thing. My shirt and my tie were all wet. I was soaked to the waist, and the collar of my jacket stank of coffee vomit. My mother took me back to the casket. I looked like someone who had partied all night and was on the verge of an alcoholic coma. The transfusions had made my father's face swell up, which gave him a disapproving pout as if in response to my hung-over look. The people began to arrive. They paid their respects, looking worried when they saw me. My mother greeted them and assured them I was fine.

At about eleven in the morning the whole Egyptian contingent of the family came directly from the airport. Despite exhaustion and I don't know how many hours of flight, their lamentations were in no way lacking in energy. They broke the silence of bereavement, and the room went from the practice of holding in pain to the art of wailing. This led to a "culture clash" which brought the police running over. Some colleagues of my father explained to them that it was an Eastern family expressing its grief and each had its own way of doing it, which reassured the police enough to put away their billy clubs. Actually, my father's family carried on this way not only because of my father's death, but especially for the way his remains were presented. Much later Athman explained to me,

"In Islam one does not dress the deceased. One undresses it from its Here and Now clothes. Naked, washed, and placed in its shroud, he is put back into the hands of God, and only those who knew him along with his family can uncover his face to ask his forgiveness before his great journey. . . ."

To dress my father in Western clothes and display him in the American way was for his family a crime against the deceased. My father's sisters scratched their cheeks with their fingernails. No one could stop them except for their husbands and their brothers, who let them do it because they too were hysterically angry. If it hadn't been their brother laid out there, my aunts would've thrown the casket with the corpse still in it on the sidewalk and into the gutter. It was at that moment that I understood that sorrow had to be managed according to a prescribed ritual. If the ritual is disturbed, sorrow can reach intolerable levels and provoke a desire for vengeance. That's why my aunts yelled in my mother's face, "We'll make you pay for this circus!"

Western holidays are Dionysian, and beauty is Apollonian, and tragedy needs both because you have to celebrate sorrow with beauty, whereas in Islam, it's totally different. Athman told me: "In Islam, a holiday is celebrating God. Death is recognizing God's power and this recognition is also celebrating God. That's why in Islam holidays and burial seem alike in their sobriety. In other beliefs, they seem alike in their pageantry. They say that the emotions aren't the same for the two. They want us to believe that tears of joy and tears of sorrow are not the same. For us, emotion and tears always have the same origin: the submission to God. Because, happy or sad, one submits to God. Our emotion is in the submission to God. What does the rest matter because it's all just context."

As for my poor mother . . . she had ordered the funeral as she would have ordered her car, her shopping. . . . Of course, she had gone through all the funeral arrangements with the funeral people, and even if she knew that she could order a Muslim funeral, she wouldn't have thought it important because she was more concerned with how to do a funeral in keeping with his exile rather than one that emphasized it. But for my father's family, seeing him in a casket in Western clothing was like compounding his exile to the extreme, because the exile of the Here and Now is temporary, but you can't exile a Muslim in his Hereafter, even if the deceased, during his life, chose to be exiled. Those in his family who live after him have to prevent his exile in the Hereafter. It's up to them to ensure that he leaves to be with his God and nowhere else.

As a result, my father's brothers contacted the embassy so that the Muslim rites could be carried out.

At the beginning of the legal paper signing, my mother was with my uncles and my father's oldest sister in one of the funeral home's offices to negotiate the disposal of her husband's remains. The oldest sister opened the hostilities:

"You had him all your life. Now that he's dead, give him back to his family."

"What family?"

"Us!"

"You? You're the family that he had. Raouf and I are the family that he made. Should he belong to the family of his birth or to the one he built?"

My aunt, speaking as a woman who had immediately grasped that religion is based on a covenant, and not on birth, answered back, "You are as much his family as we are."

"No! You are his family; we are *of him*."

My uncle, with a male arrogance and insecure about his virility to the point of being ignorant of the separation of powers in Islam, affirmed with audacity, "Where's the problem?"

"The problem is that you can't decide anything before my son and I do."

The young brother couldn't help saying without even noticing, "God cannot betray us."

With tears in her eyes, my mother sighed. "Luckily on this ground God did betray you. Otherwise, I would've lost my faith. Come Raouf, God has decided."

When we returned to my father's side, all of his colleagues from work stared at us intently and anxiously. My mother held me by the hand. It was wet and frozen. My mother controlled her outside temperature, but only God knew what storms were raging within.

When my great-aunt went to tell the rest of the family what went on, they started to cry out to God, yelling and screaming. The funeral home was shaken a second time by a seismic tremor for which it was not designed. My young aunt and one of my uncles launched into an oratorical joust, mixing verses and insults and overwhelming my mother, who held back her anger and pain out of respect for my father. She wanted a burial for him worthy of his exile. It was her way of telling everyone that he had not been all that unhappy. My mother wanted my father's American colleagues to read success into his funeral, and my father's family wanted to find in his funeral his connection to them and to Islam. They and my mother were not in the same world, in the same reality, on the same battleground.

Next to our room, some musicians were mourning the death of one of their own. The music stopped so they could come to see what was going on in our room. An Afro-American saxophonist broke into an improvisation. His instrument expressed such a sadness that everyone fell silent, including my aunts. With a swaying step he came up to my father's casket, splitting the crowd in two. He ended his improvisation with Sidney Bechet's "Little Flower." My father's family left the funeral home, the neighborhood, the city, the country without a backward glance, with anger in their step and without mourning. My mother redressed them saying, "With anger in their hearts grief goes out the door."

After they left, my mother kissed my father's forehead and said to him, "Don't worry, I'm here."

The group of his friends and colleagues stood paralyzed and dumbfounded. They hadn't finished trying to figure out what happened when the Egyptian consul made his entry, followed by the corpse washers, three men in traditional garb. They headed straight for my mother who, I felt, was in the process of calming her anger, of disinfecting the ill effects of hatred, and sterilizing her pain from the baseness of a world which had placed her at its crossroads and was tearing her in all directions. She had only one wish: to hold herself together.

The consul asked her, "Are you the spouse of the deceased?"

She answered, "Those who called for you have left. As for me, I am indeed his spouse and I don't want him touched. Please accept my apologies for the inconvenience."

"Madam, may I remind you that he is Muslim and that it is your duty as a Muslim yourself to give him a Muslim burial."

"It's not that simple!"

"Madam, I am not here to tell you what to do, but to help you and remind you that the identity of Islam is indelible."

"If it's indelible, then he'll remain a Muslim, no matter what."

"You are the responsible party in this, Madam."

"Sir, I no longer have any confidence in the Muslims of the Here and Now. I'll put it off as I see fit until the Hereafter, and I will leave it to God."

"There is a rite, Madam."

"Sir, for the forty years I've been here, I've had to pray according to my own rites, because no one came to help me give any meaning to my prayers or to have them conform to any particular ritual. Our community lived torn apart and strayed from each other. I want to bury my husband according to this reality. I will not go as far as to lie to God pretending to respect a ritual that our destiny never knew. God

will know the truth of our existence. . . . I can't understand
how we can protect *God* from our misdeeds when He is there
to protect *us* from misdeeds. The faithful who act stupidly
breathe stupidity into religion."

"My duty, Madam, is to remind you of yours and that's
all."

"I am a woman of duty! It's because your sense of duty
is masculine that we can't have the same point of view, Sir!"

"Madam, I share your sorrow but I don't understand
your hysterics."

My mother was drunk with sorrow. This drunkenness,
a mixture of dizziness and lucidity, creates a whirlwind of
words, thoughts, unexpected sentences with unknown
meanings, all capable of turning a simple discussion into an
esoteric debate. The consul continued his attack with an
ultimatum that sounded like a threat.

"What is your final decision?"

My mother looked him straight in the eyes. She had
understood that if the family's disgrace bore heavy conse-
quences, the official disgrace would have even more. She
wanted to liberate my father from exile but not from his
family. She came up with a decision, "After the civil ceremony, you will wash him and he will leave straight for the
cemetery."

The consul and his imams put themselves in a corner
of the room as if to show their disapproval in an obvious way.
My mother was invited by the officiant to speak as prescribed by protocol. She went up to the podium, and as she
inspected the room as if she were looking for God and his
angels, the technician adjusted the microphone to the height

of her mouth. Then, despite her dry mouth and body trembling from stage fright, with a sure voice and with a calm that silenced the room of the echoed cries still resounding in our heads, she said:

"Dear friends, my dear colleagues, thank you for being here. At this moment, your presence is the most reassuring thing for me. As for you, my dear Abu Raouf, at the time when I was finally going to take advantage of your presence, here I am already in the process of evoking your absence. I would have rather talked about you in the future and now I have to resign myself to talk about you in the past tense.

"I am an experimental scientist. I am neither a technician nor a philosopher, but on the basis of my experience, I would say that each of us leaves this world as he lived it. Abu Raouf loved his work and he died at work. He loved America and he died in America. He loved life and he died in the prime of life.

"Death hears our deepest desires and answers them. That is destiny. It listens to us and if we know how to be heard, it answers. I tried to listen to Abu Raouf's destiny and I tried to be faithful to it all my life up until today. I tried to listen to the deepest of what we shared together and to respond generously and equitably to our destiny as exiles.

"I love the Lebanese people who saw me born, and I am proud of it.

"I love the American people. I became one and I am proud of it. In my soul and in my conscience, I am Lebanese as much as American. I am Lebanese by birth and Lebanon is the cradle of my childhood. I am an American by conscience and America is the cradle of my renaissance as a woman and adult. I will go out of exile only when the adult and the woman that I am will be able to enjoy in all freedom the place of their childhood, only when the child I was will fully recognize herself in the woman and adult that I have become.

"This is why I cannot say that I am Lebanese, exiled in America, that I cannot affirm that America is an exile for me. Because, in fact, I am in exile from a utopian country. I am exiled from a utopia which would be a fusion of my country of birth and my adopted country. But what saves true exiles is that they develop an extraordinary energy, and if they are talented, they will be exceptional. They immerse themselves in their work so as not to have to think about their situation. Because in the final analysis they become free; no fixed career path, no prescribed social ambition, no society to look over their shoulders. Suddenly, they become exposed to the entire planet, except to their own people. Rejected by them, they are forced to make themselves heard by the world in order to be heard by their own people. Since our peoples don't have the means to live in the universal, they deliver us over to the hell of exile so that we may be universal.

"Shunned by two societies, the one we left and the one in which we arrived, we become unfettered observers of others, of ourselves, and lucidity tells us that from now on we will exist only in what we do. Work is not just a livelihood but a means of survival. That's why my dear Abu Raouf didn't survive his work.

"That's why I decided to entrust him to you for this last journey rather than to have him travel toward his family. Here he lived and here he died and here he will be buried.

You have to accept fate to the point of transforming it into legend. That's how the history of the anonymous is written. May God give you the peace of which you are worthy.

"My dear friends, I am required to change the ceremony and I apologize to those who wanted to speak. I propose that they speak at the cemetery because I have to turn Abu Raouf's body over to the three men who will prepare the remains according to Muslim rituals. After that, we'll go directly to the cemetery. Thank you for your understanding."

The casket, on its rolling carriage, was pushed away by two of the undertakers. Followed by the three body washers, they went toward the prep room. A half hour later, the consul came looking for me.

"Are you the son of the deceased?"

"Yes."

"You have to be a witness to the closing of the casket."

I went into the prep room. My father was in his casket, covered with a white shroud, the head slightly turned on its side. He smelled of musk and amber. He seemed to be sleeping peacefully. I tried to kiss him, but the imam stopped me saying, "If someone touches the body, we have to rewash it."

They put the lid on, screwed it down and, on the screw next to the head, a wax seal was affixed by one of the washers. Once he had confirmed that the wax was dry, he said to me, "He is with God now."

After a long silence, I heard Atik ask me, "Are you okay?"

I wondered why he asked me that and I said, "Yes, I'm okay, I'm just fine."

I felt as if I had just come out of a deep dream. He explained to me that he had hypnotized me in order to know where my fears were focused, which, according to him, was linked to the image of an intolerable death for me: my father's. . . .

He prescribed a series of pills whose names I don't know because he just put them into an unlabeled pill bottle. Then he said to me, "This'll help you get over the moments of anxiety and, in particular, you'll be able to overcome all panic situations. And now say again with me the oath: 'In the name of God the Merciful. I swear in the name of God:

'SAY: God is He, the Unique.
God. The Supreme refuge.
He begot none nor was He begotten.
None could be His equal or like.' (S112)

'BY God, we shall not sell our testament at any price, not even to a near relative, nor shall we conceal the testimony of God, for then we should surely be amongst criminals.' (S5, V106)

'PRAISE be to God, Lord and Master of all worlds. The Merciful in essence and in excellence. Master of the Day of Judgment. It is You whom we adore! And it is from You that we implore aid. Guide us on the straight path. The path of those whom You have touched with Your grace, and not of those who have incurred Your wrath, not of those who have gone astray.' (S1)

"And our great imam Abu Talib al-Makki teaches us: 'Patience is a duty and a virtue at the same time, depending on if it's an order or an obligation.'"

"Why are you telling me this?"

"Because, in your case, it is a virtue."

"I would've preferred that it be out of duty."

"It's a credit to you. You can go back to your room and rest now."

After sunset prayers, the guide spoke to us about angels:

"Omar ibn al-Khattab recounts that one day while he was seated in the company of the Prophet, a traveler introduced himself to them and asked the following question of the Prophet:

"'What is faith?'

"The Prophet answered thus: *'Faith is believing in God, in angels, in the revealed Books, in the last day of reckoning be it good or bad.'*

"These are the beliefs on which the Muslim faith is built. The Prophet, in answering this traveler, placed the angels in second place before the Books and before himself. Because simply without angels, there would have been neither Books nor Prophets. Thus believing in angels is part of our faith.

"Who are the angels? How many are there? And what do they do? The angels are beings of light, capable of appearing in all forms and no one knows their number. God said,

'No one knows the armies of your Lord.' (S74, V31)

"As for their functions, they are multiple and varied. There are messengers like the archangel Gabriel who was given the charge by God to transmit the revelation to the Prophet.

"There are scribes, those who record all our actions looking to the last judgment. It is said,

'HE [man] doesn't pronounce a word without having near him an observer to inscribe it.' (S50, V18)

"There are those charged with carrying the Throne. God says,

'ON that day eight angels will bear above them the Throne of your Lord.' (S69, V17)

"There are those guardians who watch over. God said,

'HE [man] has angels who are before him and behind him and who watch over him by God's order.' (S13, V11)

'WE have appointed only angels as guardians of hell.' (S74, V31)

"And finally there are two angels responsible for interrogating the dead in their tomb. This multitude of angels is dedicated, in addition to the functions assigned to each of them, to God's exaltation. It is said,

'THE angels exalt the glory of God and His purity night and day endlessly.' (S21, V20)

"Angels, and herein lies their importance and supreme quality, disobey none of God's orders. Execution is immediate and certain. It is said,

'O YOU who believed! Put yourself, you and yours, in the shelter of a fire having as fuel rocks and humans, guarded by stern and severe angels who never disobey God in what He commands them and they do strictly what He orders them.' (S66, V6)

'THEY [the angels] never speak before Him and act on His command.' (S21, V27)

"Thus the angels are neither superior nor inferior to man. They are near to God in their obedience, and whosoever cultivates in himself obedience, and whosoever increases and deepens his obedience, is closer to God and multiplies the number of angels who protect him and who will accompany him in his deeds. If angels are beings of light, submitting to God is receiving this light to a point that you will be similar to angels. The key to your success is in your obedience and the key to your obedience is in your faith. By obeying, one increases his faith because having faith is accepting to obey.

"He who makes the decision to fight on the path of God and be a Martyr in God's cause must be the equal of the angels in obedience, and they will be for him the best guardians.

'AND even more! If you are patient and you fear God, and the enemies assail you heedlessly, your Lord will reinforce you with five thousand of His warrior angels carrying distinctive signs.' (S3, V125)

"May peace be with you."

The two weeks of work were fascinating. Fouad, Omar, and Safar were exciting people, and showed me ways of being that I had never known before: powerful personalities with a limitless determination. They said that at each moment of the operation you had to choose the most subtle, the most intelligent, and the most unexpected solution, and that's how we could guarantee the success of the action.

That's how, at the end of two weeks, we had perfected the theoretical and practical aspects of the overall operation. If it succeeded, it would be a marvel of invention, a technical feat and a unique spectacle. It would be our gift to God.

El Afghani, coming to get me for sunset prayers, reminded me that it was our last night here and that I had to take my last will and testament with me to read.

When I arrived in the big room, the others were already there. It's been more than three weeks since we've seen each other here at sunset for regular prayers and straightforward speeches. On this day, for the first time, I felt doubts hovering and anxiety creeping in. Everything we had struggled against for weeks returned like a fog which enveloped this last meeting. El Yemeni, who was usually satisfied to signal the hour of prayer to the guide without acting as the muezzin, carried away by the atmosphere, did a call to prayer, whose sad yet powerful singing restored all certainty. "God is Great" sung by him expelled doubt from our hearts, from our bodies, and from our meeting. His voice undulated between low and high pitch with an exceptional facility that touched the divine. Within a few moments and in a single call he made the beauty, the grandeur, and the generosity of God come to life for us. He banished sadness from our hearts and chased away all the *shaytan* from the room and the *jinn* who would have come in.

When the guide got up to lead the prayer, his first "God is great" was an everyday one, because, according to what I had understood, in no case should this last day seem special or different. We went on, continuing on the same path, toward the same goal, and every day was both exceptional and ordinary. After the prayer and the *du'a*, the special supplication, the jurist told us, "Before you turn over your final will and testament to us, I ask you to read it out loud and with an uncovered face. We will be your witnesses."

Fouad began. He undid the shroud from his head and let it fall on his shoulders like a hood. As we were lined up side by side, I could scarcely see his profile. He removed a sheet of paper from an envelope and, in a serious but neutral voice, began to read:

"In the name of God the Merciful. Fouad, faithful son, poor servant of God. It is written in the Holy Book:

> 'MY prayer, my devotion, my life and my death belong to God, Master of the universe. None is equal to Him. This is what has been commanded of me, I am the first of the Muslims.' (S6, V162–163)

"This is what I believed, what I believe, and what I shall believe forever. So, you, my brothers in Islam, my family, my friends, do not go looking to understand either why or how. Things are simple. Our duty is to answer God. He commands it, and with His help, we have done it. God teaches us:

> 'WE shall put you to the test by fear, famine, loss of wealth in your life and your crops. And announce the good news to the patient. Those who say, when adversity strikes them: "To God we belong and to Him we return."' (S2, V155–56)

"Truth is in the word of God.

"Peace be with you."

Fouad calmly refolded the sheet of paper, put it back in the envelope, and handed it to the jurist.

Then Safar took his turn, uncovered his face, and read:

"In the name of God the Merciful. Safar, faithful son, weak servant of God Almighty. God said to His Prophet the day of his last pilgrimage:

> "TODAY those who have renounced lose hope of turning you away from your Religion. Fear them not. Fear Me. Today I have completed and given to you your perfect Religion; I have granted you My grace and My benefit and I decree Islam as your Religion.' (S5, V3)

"If God wanted Islam for humanity, humanity must become Muslim. We strive to enforce that law, for God's commandments are clear and indisputable. And our Prophet tells us: '*Whosoever is killed defending his possessions is a Martyr.*' My only possession is Islam! And I want to defend it.

'To God we belong and to Him we return.' (S2, V156)

"God speaks the truth.

"Peace be with you."

Next it was Athman's turn:
"In the name of God the Merciful. Athman, faithful son. Humble servant of God, Muslim by filiation and by conviction and combatant in God's cause, Martyr if God wills it.

"To those whom, among the Islamic *Ummah*, still have a confused mind and blurry vision, shaken by the mental poverty of this world and who have lost their bearings, to those I say: our action will be as the black stone of the Kaaba, a landmark to which, in the future, all Muslims will return. Our act may seem crazy, granted, but it is the appropriate reply to a world gone crazy. My father, may God rest his soul, used to tell me: 'Never speak intelligently to idiots. If they were intelligent, they wouldn't be idiots.' I give my life to the glory of God and against the idiotic injustice of this world.

'To God we belong and to Him we return.' (S2, V156)

"God is great.

"Peace be with you."

When I freed my face and my head from the shroud and hood, directly in the sight of the guide and of the others, I felt as if I were taking a bandage off a face whose identity was sick, a severe burn victim who felt almost all healed and cured. I read my last words in the tone of a convalescent:

"In the name of God the Merciful. Raouf, faithful son.

"I don't know how my mother lived, I don't know how my father died, and I ended up understanding that I didn't have any existence. And, yet, . . . I followed the path of an easy life, made up of success guaranteed by a society which programmed me to succeed without any surprises. But this wasn't the right path. My father's death led me to question myself about my birth and my own death.

"If I volunteered in the *jihad* to become a Martyr, it's to come to grips with my death by offering it to God and to sublimate my fallen birth in order to be reborn in virtue. Being born and living in the shadow of history and dying as a Martyr is a way of stealing the light of the Here and Now to offer it as a bouquet to God in the Hereafter. When God said:

'AND here comes the intoxication of death at the same time as truth. It is this that you always tried to avert.' (S50, V19)

I felt that He was speaking almost directly to me.

"God is great.

"Peace be with you."

I took my turn in handing over my envelope to the jurist. Then it was Omar's turn. When he took off his hood and his shroud for the first time, I recognized the Pakistani from the Daddy-O Club.

"In the name of God the Merciful. Omar, faithful son.

"God is great, God is great, God is great!

"I witness that He is the One and that Muhammad is His Prophet. God is great. I didn't decide to die. I didn't decide to destroy myself. God, in His greatness, decided that I be a Martyr in His cause and in the cause of Muslims worldwide. Such is my destiny. You, my family, you, my friends, don't cry. Cry for yourselves!

"God is great!

"Peace be with you."

Then he gave his envelope to the jurist.

A silence settled in when each of us recited the *Fatiha* and the oath to ourselves, after which the guide spoke with serenity, calm, and satisfaction: "Our Prophet said to his grandson, Hasan ibn Ali: '*Leave behind whatever causes doubt in you for that which stirs no doubt in you.*'

"With God's help, everything is accomplished and brought to fruition with a simplicity and facility that proves this action is truly desired by God. You've found answers to theoretical problems that many of their engineers don't find. You have carried out calculations of great complexity and thanks to God, they've become clear. The *fatwa* of our imams, of our fathers, has come at the right time. As for you, you are already radiant. You carry in you the light of sincere Martyrs. You are already under the protection of God.

"Yesterday, I had a dream. I was standing at the front door of the house we are at, and, one by one, you left the house. I saw you come toward the door accompanied by four angels, two on your right shoulder and two on your left shoulder. When you opened the door to leave, you were struck by an intense light and when the last of you closed the door, I remained in the dark, blinded by this light.

"This dream has two important meanings: the first is that God has taken you under His benediction and the second is that those who remain behind you in this world Here and Now have been blinded by God so that you remain undetected. God is protecting you already. Even from me!

"Know also that your action is an operation which consists of five essential steps:

The first is the moment preceding your departure from your homes.

The second is the path toward the place of the action.

The third is the space which precedes the place of action.

The fourth is the very place of action itself.

The fifth is your arrival at God's side.

How great is God's mercy and how transcendent is His harmony!

These five steps are also the five pillars of Islam:
Before leaving, you will bear witness.

"The path is nothing other than prayer for the success of your action.

"When you are at the airport, this will be the difficult stage where you will be put to the test. At this time your Ramadan will not be the fast of abstinence from food and drink; it will be your abstinence from fear and panic. At that time you will know that you have done Ramadan your whole life to educate your stomach, your desires, your longings, and this will serve to dominate your senses and your nerves to achieve, with God's help, the necessary control at the right time.

"When you're in the airplane, you will accomplish the fourth step, which is the equivalent of the *zakat*, almsgiving based on your wealth. But this time you will become the wealth and you will constitute the almsgiving. God multiplies the wealth of those who give God's share as *zakat*. As for you who are going to give your life as *zakat*, God will repay you with a better life.

"The fifth step is the pilgrimage to the holy places. When the plane reaches its target, you will be at the holy places of God, which means in the hands of God. This will be your pilgrimage. At the moment you act, you will be the greatest pilgrims who will transform a profane place into a holy place.

"The five steps of your action also correspond to the five daily prayers:

"The sunrise prayer that you do upon waking up in your house. That is the first step.

"The midday prayer that you do at your workplace is the second step of your path.

"The afternoon prayer, decisive for your day's piety, corresponds to your arrival at the airport. That's the third step.

"The fourth prayer, the sunset prayer, is that of your redemption when you make up for the missed prayers of the day, and which concludes your day. It corresponds to your fourth location, the plane, which means the action.

"Finally, the fifth prayer, the evening one, the one just before sleep. This one, if all goes well and with God's help, you will do in Paradise with all the other Martyrs of Islam.

"What happiness, my brothers, to climb these five steps and to be in the eternal House, God's House! Five steps which symbolize the five pillars of Islam, the five prayers and the five hundred thousand billion miseries suffered by Muslims of the world.

'FIGHT them so that God may punish and dishonor them at your hands. He will give you victory over them and heal the hearts of a believing people.' (S9, V14)

"During these five steps, you will think of only three things: of God, of the *action*, and of your constant *supplications*.

"When you rise in the morning, you will say the morning supplication:

'Praise be to Allah Who brought us back to life after having us die. It is He who gives resurrection! Praise be to Allah Who gives good health to my body, and who gave me my soul and allowed me to invoke His name.'

"At the time you get dressed, don't forget to put a part of the shroud against your body and adjust your clothes so they don't get in the way during the action. Then, you will say the supplication of clothing:

'O my Lord! All praise to You: You have dressed me in this clothing. I request of You its benefit and the benefit for which it has been made, and I implore refuge beside You against its harm and the harm for which it was made.'

"Before going out, redo your ablutions. The angels accompanying you will pray for you and protect you as long as you are purified. Then say the supplication for going out of the house:

'In the name of Allah, I place my confidence in Allah. There is no power or force except by Allah's grace. O Allah! I take refuge beside You so as not to get lost or go astray, be wrong or be wronged, commit an injustice or wrongdoing or undergo the injustice of another.'

"When you are in the taxi or in your car, you will say the supplication of travel and upon entering a city:

'IN the name of God the Merciful. Glory to Him who has subjected this to us while we were not capable of overcoming it. It is to our Lord that we shall return. (S43, V13–14)

'All Praise to Allah, Allah is Great. I was unjust unto myself,
absolve me. None can pardon sins but You! O Allah! Lord of
the seven heavens and of everything they cover, Lord of the
seven earths and everything they contain, Lord of the devils
and of all the faithful that they lead astray, and Lord of the
winds and of everything they scatter! I implore You to accord
me the generosity of this city, the generosity of its inhabitants,
and the generosity of what it holds and I take refuge beside
You against its wrongdoing, the wrongdoing of its inhabitants
and the wrongdoing that it holds.'

"When you arrive at the airport, you will say the supplication of place:

'God, I request from You the best of this place and protection
against its evils. There is no God but Allah, the Only One,
without any peer, all praise and sovereignty to Him. He brings
life, death, and He is the Living One who does not die.
Goodness is in His hands and He is the Omnipotent.'

"Dear Martyrs,
"You must be calm, smiling, and you must look relaxed
in the airport. If necessary, light up a cigarette and be by
yourself in the smoking section. In your hearts, and without anyone noticing, say:

'Now God has lightened your burden and He
found out that there are weaknesses in you. If you
group one hundred stouthearted men together,

they will vanquish two hundred, and if you total one thousand, they will vanquish two thousand with the help of God, and God is with those that persevere. (S8, V66)

'Do not weaken in the confrontation with these people; if you suffer, they will suffer as much as you. But you will have hope from God and they will hope not.' (S4, V104)

"When you reach your departure gate, take a newspaper and pretend to be reading it while reciting in your hearts without others' noticing you:

'O Allah! There are no other omens than Yours, no other benefits than Yours, and no other God than You, the Great, the All-Merciful. There is no divinity but Allah, Lord of the immense Throne. There is no divinity but Allah, Lord of the heavens, of the earth, and of the Noble Throne. By the holy words of Allah which no virtuous or perverse one can surpass, I take refuge from the evil of these creatures, from their offspring, and from the evil that has spread on the earth, from the evil which falls from the sky, from the evil which goes up to the sky, from the evil which comes out of the earth, from the plots which are hatched night and day and from the evil of all visitors except those that visit for good purpose. O All-Merciful!'

'Allah, Allah, my Lord; I can think of nothing like Him. O Allah! We put You in their throats and we take refuge beside

You from their wrongdoings. O Allah! You are my support
and my defender. It is You that I champion, and it is for You
that I do battle. O Allah, You are the Lord of the immense
Throne! Be my Protector against all unbelievers, and against
their like among Your creatures so that no one among them
may deceive me or do me wrong. Glory is Your glory, protection is Your protection. Majestic are Your praises, and there is
no divinity except You.

'Allah is Greater and more Precious than all His creations.
Allah is more Powerful than everything that frightens or scares
me. I take refuge beside Allah outside of Whom there is no
other divinity. He is the One Who holds up the seven heavens
so that they fall not to earth without His permission. I take
refuge from the evil of Your servant, from his soldiers and
partisans and allies among whom count human beings and *jinn*.
O Allah! Protect me against their wrongdoing. There is no
other divinity but You.'

"When you are in the plane, say the travel supplication
again:

'O Allah! We implore You to grant us charity and piety in this
particular voyage. O Allah! Facilitate our travel and shorten its
distance. O Allah! You are our Companion on this trip and
Successor in the family. O Allah! I take refuge beside You
against the disaster of the trip, from the looks of horror and
changes for the worse in possessions and family.'

'O Allah, Revealer of the Book and prompt settler of accounts!
Vanquish the wrongdoers. O Allah! Vanquish them and shake
them up. O Allah, defend me from them by Your will.'

"Concentrate on the action and remember that you are doing battle for the love of God and especially that you are very close to Him, that very little time separates you from your arrival at God's side. When the plane takes off, you'll have to be ready to act. So you'll have to be exacting in your gestures, and efficient in carrying out the plan.

"At this moment none will exist for himself. You will all be for God, and you will act according to the teachings of God and of His Prophet. In the way that you act, you will be recognized as Martyrs of Islam.

"You will begin the battle crying *"Allahu Akbar"* ("God is great"). You will say verses of the Koran out loud to fill the passengers' hearts with fear. May the word of God freeze and paralyze them.

"Then strike with strength and respect the instructions of the Prophet, who said:

'GOD prescribes the act well done in all things. Thus if you kill, kill appropriately and if you slaughter, do it with care; let the blade be honed and let the beast be spared suffering.'

"You should encourage each other with the words of God.

'ON the point of battling Goliath and his army, they cried: "Lord, arm us with patience, strengthen our steps, and give us victory over this unbelieving people."' (S2, V250)

"After, you will all find yourselves in the highest realm of heaven, God willing. It is He who tells us:

'O calmed soul!
Return to your Lord satisfied and pleased.
Enter among my servants.
And enter into my Paradise.' (S89, V27–30)

"Dear Martyrs,

"Tomorrow each of you will return to his normal life. For God, for us, and for the planet's Muslims, you are ready to act, and God is ready to grant you His Mercy. We strongly recommend that you follow the path of conduct which has been taught you from the time that you first received the order to act.

"You will prepare yourself first by shaving your private parts. You will purify your body by performing both simple and complete ablutions and you will perfume yourself.

'THOSE who take God, His apostle, and the Faithful as protectors, are like God's militia; victory is theirs.' (S5, V56)

"You will renew your intention of dying for the love of God. You will redo your oath for yourselves. You will pray and persevere in prayer asking God to give you victory. It is He Who hears and Who knows all. And say:

'ALLAH is enough for us; He is our best protector.'
(S3, V173)

"You will read and recite out loud suras and verses that will be indicated to you, in particular, the suras *Al-Anfal* ('Spoils') and *Al-Tawbah* ('Return to God') which are the spiritual and legal path of conduct of God's Martyrs and warriors.

"Absorb your mind in thought about God, and the best way of thinking about God is to read and reread the Koran. Purify your soul and forget the Here and Now. Think of the Hereafter, of your coming to God, and you will be at peace. You will feel the calm of the great Martyrs.

"Remind your soul of submission. Whatever the circumstances may be, your soul should answer with obedience, and remember that you are not doing combat against yourselves, but against the heathens, and for God. And it's to Him that you will return.

"Tell your mind about resolution and determination, and tell yourself that what's happening to you is inevitable because it's God's decision. Remind yourself that it's the greatest and most beautiful test to which God puts you in order to be called to Him and to absolve your sins and those of your parents and seventy-two others closest to you.

"Think of your life, of all the time you wasted amusing yourself, in thinking without any results, in thinking without acting. On this day, God will give you the chance to act without thinking. The action will necessarily be, thanks to you, purified of all thoughts of failure which could prevent it from being carried out to the very end. For that you will have to put your confidence in God. The imam Ali ibn Abi Talib says: 'The Here and Now left turning its back on the Hereafter which advances. To each his filiation. Be the sons of the Hereafter and not the sons of the Here and Now, for today you can act without being judged, while tomorrow you will be judged without being able to act.'

"Think of all your brother Muslims scattered throughout the world, destitute and dishonored.

"Review the action plan and pay attention to the slightest detail. Imagine all possible difficulties and come up with appropriate responses. Arm your mind with solutions.

"At the moment you receive the specifics of the day and hour of the action, you will be at the thirty-third hour of the operation. Why thirty-three hours? Because the number 33 is the key to mysteries. It's the number of beads in our prayer beads and 33x2=66=Allah.

"Thirty-three hours, the half of Allah's numerical value, will symbolize the halfway point left to you in your life before meeting God, and He will accompany you on the other half toward Paradise.

"In the course of these thirty-three hours, your shoulders will be weighed down, not by fear of dying or the anxiety of passing away. What to you will look like fear will be nothing but an immense adoration, carrying the weight and anger of two billion despised Muslims and Palestinians crushed by Jews, while our corrupt little kings bathe in luxury like Hindus bathe in the Ganges. You will think of that God who imagined us the best among nations, and who now finds us the worst of the class, the dunces among nations and the first in emigration. Our Prophet only chose exile to Medina, convinced of a triumphant return to Mecca. During these thirty-three hours you will be raised to the rank of the Companions of the Prophet. You will be Abu Bakr, Ali, Omar, Khalid ibn al-Walid, and Hamza, the beloved Companions of the Prophet. You will be *buraq*, the winged horse of the Prophet, who transported him to Jerusalem. You will all be the *buraq* of iron and of fire, bearers of God's punishment. You should know that the moment you board the plane, the passengers who will be there won't be normal passengers, despite their appearance. They will really be human forms which embody the souls of the greatest Martyrs of Islam such as Jamal al-Din al-Afghani, Salah al-Din al-Ayubi, all who will have left Paradise to be with you in this operation. That's why if one of you backs off or quits at the decisive moment, he will have abandoned and betrayed the great Martyrs of Islam. For, on this day, on the plane, you will be a multitude of Muslim souls, at peace, and you will be the very soul of Islam in the world.

"The death of all the passengers is necessary to liberate the souls of our Martyrs. You are, by the choice of your action, at the gates of Paradise. Once the action is accomplished, God will welcome you, surrounded by all the Martyrs, into Paradise.

"For all these reasons, the choice of the day selected will be a difficult choice, because we have to synchronize the divine conditions which surround the action and the material and technical conditions which define the action. With the help of God we will watch out that all the conditions necessary for the success of the action be consolidated. With the help of God, we are going to remember the oath."

Then the guide began the oath:

"The only brothers you know are in the faith. The Koran is your only memory. Islam is your sole source."

We all repeated out loud after the guide: "That is true, God is Powerful."

"Power over oneself is the most beautiful and difficult thing. One's power is strengthened by faith in God."

"That is true, God is Powerful."

"True power is the one which answers God through submission and answers men through His truth."

"That is true, God is Powerful."

"Power must pass from one believer to another in the serenity of learning and in the submission to God."

"That is true, God is Powerful."

"The real power of God is difficult to assume because it is difficult to uphold in its truth."

"That is true, God is Powerful."

"Powers which are born scorning religion must disappear."

"That is true, God is Powerful."

"All transition from one level of power to another is done by the test of death, and death is in the hands of God."

"That is true, God is Powerful."

"If you are afraid, death will be victorious. Death must not make you afraid. It is a call from God and he who is called by God is a fortunate man."

"That is true, God is Powerful."

"Your integrity is your only chance. And don't forget that to be in possession of oneself is not to avoid death, death being inevitable, but simply to no longer fear it."

"That is true, God is Powerful."

"When one fights for God's glory, it's God that counts the dead, not us."

"That is true, God is Powerful."

"BY God, we shall not sell our testament at any price, not even to a near relative, nor shall we conceal the testimony of God, for then we should surely be amongst criminals." (S5, V106)

"That is true, God is Powerful."

"My brothers, you just completed a month of preparation and purification. We cleansed your body and your mind with the word of God. With God's help, we have made men-angels of you, men already in the hands of God. Tomorrow, when I shall see you leave, I will be, may God forgive me, jealous. I will feel abandoned and forsaken. Your absence will add another exile to my exile, knowing you to be in the hands of God, and me, left having to wait for God's decision. I'm afraid of becoming impatient, believe me. My happiness is to find you at God's side soon. From now on, I will live only with this expectation. Let us now separate in peace and in faith. Tomorrow we will do the sunrise prayers together. You will continue to abstain from communicating or speaking amongst yourselves. You will leave this location in the order that has been indicated to you.

'O Allah! By Your knowledge of the occult and Your power over creatures, leave me alive as long as You know life is better for me, and take my soul if You know that death is better for me.

"Peace be with you."

Upon waking, I folded up my shroud and put it in a plastic bag and I continued to read what I had left to read in the Koran. Considering my reading speed, I was a little bit behind, but in spite of that I was proud of myself, given my level in Arabic.

El Afghani came to tell me that I would leave here at ten o'clock to return home. In the car that took me back, I drifted into a child's sleep, lulled by the drone of the motor and the almost imperceptible voices of parents talking. It was nice out, and the sun teased my eyes as it darted in and out through trees and clouds following the curves in the road, showing me the story of a trip as if through the end of a kaleidoscope without the colored glass pieces.

I was so relieved not to be fearful of death anymore. . . . But I feared that this feeling might be due to the medical treatment and not to the elimination of my anxiety through psychological means. What's certain is that I was feeling good about myself in every way, and nothing was more important than being in this action to the very end.

In this beginning of autumn the forests are enchanting with their colors of varied hues. When we used to go mushroom hunting, my father would say, "This is the most beautiful season because God painted it. Winter is the most covered season, summer is the most undressed season, and spring is the most nourishing."

The driver lit a cigarette whose odor woke me up. I don't know why, but I said to him, "Didn't you quit smoking?"

"I tried several times and I'm still trying, but I'm only a driver, God will forgive me. . . . That's for sure."

V

"In the name of God the All-Merciful"
From Raouf to his brother in Islam, Jamal.

Dear brother, you who know, I'm letting you know.

The day when I received and felt within me the weight of my repentance, I listened to the recording of the simple sermon that was given to me as a birthday gift as a kind of a joke. I don't know whether it's because it had something to do with my birthday, or because it spoke of the suffering of our times, but each time after listening to it I came face to face with the problematic nature of my birth: "To what end was I born?" This question appeared with such urgency that I felt myself confronted by all of the gaps in my knowledge at once. The only answer that made any sense at that moment was that in order to understand my birth, I perhaps needed to undergo a rebirth.

To be born is to be reborn, and to be reborn requires killing off what one is. That's how it all started. We cannot accept our first birth as unique and definitive since God designed it so that this first birth is only a step toward the second.

But progression through death is not man's choice for himself, for then it would be suicide. Death is God's decision. It is He who knows the hour, the day, and the manner. Rebirth depends on this first death. I believed in that and I had faith in my rebirth through God. That's why I came back to God in order to be able to find my other life through death.

As I am writing to you at this moment, I feel myself at that juncture. On the way back from my walk, I recalled three verses which confirm our action. Tomorrow, at the very moment when I pass into the other life, the inhabitants of the planet, regardless of their time zone, will all turn on their TVs at the same moment to view the event. Under the eye of the entire planet and in total anonymity, I'll make my way toward my peaceful and tranquil rebirth. I will begin my new life in the hands of God and in the face of the world. Isn't that the most beautiful gift that God could give to one of His humble servants?

I reread the three verses to familiarize myself with them again. I recited them to impregnate myself with them, and I chanted them to pump me up and invigorate me.

"In the name of God the All-Merciful"
"If We let man taste the slightest effects of Our mercy and then We strip him of it, he will truly lapse into despair and dejection." (S11, V9)

"ONLY those who have patience and do good
works will have Our pardon and a great reward."
(S11, V11)
"THEY sold off God's verses for a pitiful price and
then they chased the others far from His sight. It
is truly evil what they did." (S9, V9)

Before, for me, the path was laid out. God and His
Prophet were my signposts, but the path itself was uncertain.
I knew nothing about Islam, but I felt everything about it.
Today, for me, Islam has become more than a religion, more
than an identity. It's a defining religion which offers me a
battle to fight, a necessary aspect for me. I wrapped my body
in religious practices and I opened my chest to God, Who then
opened my heart. I sublimated my imperfections through
prayer. I distanced myself from all sin so that my repentance
was gratuitous. But since I wished to remain humble, I baptized this repentance my "repentance of pride," so that I had
to seek forgiveness for my vanity and remain the human that
God destined us all to be. I retrained myself in every way:
how to sit, stand, laugh. . . . My body was foreign to me; I
began to recognize it and to inscribe it into the tradition of
the Prophet. My laugh had changed. For someone who never
managed to finish a sentence before, I learned to complete
each one thanks to my recitation of the Koran, because you
can't leave the verses of God suspended in midair. I also
learned to finish everything that I asked to be put on my plate,
and to finish reading what I started.

It's late at night. I'm prepared and I've read the verses
that were indicated and that I was supposed to know by heart.

"WE took revenge upon them. We annihilated
these two cities; they serve as a striking example
to man." (S15, V79)

"TELL them: 'If out of all humans, Paradise is re-
served for you at the side of God, then dare to wish
for death, if you are sincere.'" (S2, V94)

"YOU embed night within day and day within night,
You make life emerge from death and death from
life. You award Your blessings to whom You
choose however extravagantly You wish." (S3, V27)

"WHEREVER you are, death will find you. It would
find you even in the highest of towers. Should the
unbelievers be blessed with good fortune, they say:
'This comes from God.' Should they encounter misfortune, they cry out: 'This comes from you, O
Muhammad!' Tell them: 'Everything comes from
God.' How is it that such people cannot understand
any language?" (S4, V78)

"HE who leaves home to journey in exile toward
God and His Prophet and dies on the way, his
reward is in the hands of God. God is Mercy and
Forgiveness." (S4, V100)

It is absolutely true that reading the Koran can calm
and stimulate at the same time. Each time I experience a
new awareness. Rereading helps me see what I missed, and
sheds light on what escaped me before. Rereading is like
a breeze which revives lost perfumes, forgotten scents.
At those moments, I feel the oneness of my body and soul.
My body through the sensuality of words, rhythms, and

breathing, and my soul, flattered to hear so much wisdom in each breath, struggles to grasp its import and ends up by understanding. A soul that has understood is a soul at peace.

I didn't sleep and I won't be sleeping, but I don't feel tired. I realize that those who do little are the ones who tire. For those who strive beyond their limits, fatigue is no longer a part of their thinking. It's obsolete.

I don't experience fatigue because for several weeks now I've been fasting in anticipation of the action. Under the supervision of my guide, I cleansed my body of all traces of abuse. Today I performed my simple ablutions and I broke my fast with a glass of milk and a few dates. My body has learned to function with a minimum of energy and to be satisfied with little in everything: food, water, sleep. I have lost all excess weight. When I walk, I feel everything in balance on my legs, and my muscles have just the right amount of energy to move my body without taxing my breathing or putting pressure on my joints. I feel perfectly clean on the inside and beautiful on the outside, even if beauty is only for God. We are in His image and our duty as believers is to be beautiful and clean to honor Him.

I don't feel tired because I've cut myself off from everything. The only encounter that preoccupied me was the one with myself. You can't imagine to what extent I felt like a stranger unto myself, exiled from myself, because of the way our fathers forced us to smile at idiots and to mistrust simple and honest people. They forced us into exile from our true feelings and we became misfits.

Once you get away from all that, you relax . . . which is why I sleep deeply but not for very long, so that I wake up rested and ready to go for a long time. I rid myself of dreams in my sleep by staying awake longer and longer. Dreams in sleep are the luxury of those who are unconscious. How can you sleep when the dream is right there waiting to become reality? I caught myself dreaming about how to dream my dream. Isn't that what transcendence is about? How could I make my soul's journey in this ordinary dream link up with the ultimate *barzakh*? I will slip directly into the great dream of a dead man resuscitated for the glory of God.

Since the very beginning, in my approach, I understood it was this link-up that I had to accomplish, like the planes that refuel others in midair, both in motion. In order to achieve transcendence, it was necessary to have this energy source available while in movement and to recognize that this energy was faith. I think I've done too much math. Even my most insignificant dreams slalom in and out of equations and theorems, in search of a clear path. For example, if I feel like buying a pair of jeans on the spot, the price pops into my brain and sets up possibilities: Do I have shirts in my wardrobe to go with them? And what about shoes? What started out as a little dream turns into a problem to be solved with great logical reasoning. I really wish that I could have just bought the jeans and then said later: "I did a dumb thing," with the dumb thing being the proof of my freedom to dream. Dreams considered according to every-one else's norms are no longer dreams. How can you consider a very stupid thing as an example of an uninhibited dream? I always dreamed of being a free dreamer in the same sense as being a free thinker. As soon as I understood that in Islam to die, to dream, to sleep, and to be awake were like the four corners in the impossibility of squaring the circle, I knew that I would be in my element, that Islam would be my religion, and that I was going to escape the rational linearity of time. There is a time for everything: a time to dream, a time to sleep, a time to die. Some even pushed this absurdity to the point of giving a time for time like a kind of wart on time itself. It would be like saying you have to add flesh on top of flesh.

Things between Jenny and me were starting to go bad. As I began to understand where my destiny was taking me, she seemed more and more vulgar to me, and I seemed more and more austere, distant, and coldhearted to her. In point of fact, it was simply that God had given me a new approach to life designed to prepare me to enter His kingdom, and it made me unbearable to Jenny. She remained wedded to the pleasures of the devil's pact that had brought us together. I fed my patience with mercy and peace in order to make it easier for her to accept our separation without making her suffer or causing arguments because I hate violence. I carry out what God commands of me; He alone knows what violence sustains my act.

If you want a good laugh, I could tell you about how I never enjoyed the feeling on my fingertips when I would touch women's genitals, especially in the dark. As soon as I would put my hand between their thighs, the sticky wetness of matted pubic hair made me feel like I had put my hand in a spider's nest. All the more so because Muslim women are supposed to shave their pubic hair. I could only get past that feeling if I kept the light on and stared straight into their eyes to remind me of where my hand was. I don't know why I'm telling you all of this . . . but I think that I need to be writing it down. In any case, I don't know whether I'll mail this letter tomorrow, and if I do mail it, I won't be around for you to laugh at me. Here again, Islam has helped me. I learned, in fact, that it was a spider that saved the Prophet's life during his journey of exile from Mecca to Medina, and I've had more sympathy for spiders ever since. It helped me get over my revulsion.

I have to admit that Jenny also helped me quite a bit. When I left her, I felt that I abandoned my sexuality. All of the other women I knew before her were failures for me. She's the only one whose natural reserve transcended nakedness, whose tenderness veiled the silliness of our positions and whose submission to a certain aggressiveness transcended violence. She would wrap herself in a veil of pleasure and express her orgasm with a smile. Separation from her is a tremendous rupture in my life. She was the sponge that absorbed so many of my complexes. Like a trainer, she wiped away my shame.

"She could have been the link between my former life when I was a *Jahilite* among *Jahilites* and my life today, because it was during those special moments making love to Jenny that I felt God's presence above us. I'm convinced that each of us has another half created just for us somewhere in the world. But the randomness of birth means that the girl next door will not necessarily turn out to be your other half, your matching image. Jenny is truly my other half, the one that matches me perfectly. Too bad she's a Christian! I was lucky to have her in my life. Maybe that's why I neglected my faith. By her presence, she made sense of my existence, she cured all my allergies, she freed my emotions from conflict. I lived my life as an engineer knowing that I could devote myself entirely to my career, because the other problems in life had found their perfect solutions. Consequently, I wound up speaking a cybernetic language. I was the extension of a machine that was gradually becoming a prosthesis for me. Jenny and I were so much like two halves of a whole that in bed we became one. We made love as two, of course, but it was only an act of solitary masturbation. Our relationship was so perfect and our life so well tuned that we were fulfilled in every way imaginable. But this fulfillment was in itself a limitation, something that I had always called satisfaction.

I was a satisfied man. This satisfaction filled my life the way light, billowy stuffing fills a cushion and prevents us from feeling our buttocks on a chair or our sleeping head on a pillow. This happiness worried me. I concluded that meeting up with the ideal person was not necessarily ideal. Love needs difference.

When the imam said in his sermon during the *Eid*, "Be wary of the Here and Now," I understood that this cushion was life here on earth. Whether the "here" is here or elsewhere, the Here and Now exists and is not to be trusted.

What worried me in this whole thought process was the fact that my parents' existence had no place in it, not because my mother didn't know about my activities, but because their nonexistence in my mind alarmed me at times. What I was doing then was neither for nor against them, it was neither to please nor displease them.

They became increasingly removed from the picture with each step I took forward in this process. I was surprised at not feeling this detachment, this autonomy in relation to my parents, who were a real absence in my process of reconstructing the remains of a religious faith left in shreds that I had inherited from them. As exiles, their faith was divided between different values. It was a faith that they never quite knew what to do with, despite their intellect and social status. And, yet, they were specialists of expertise. . . . They truly had their own way of making sense of things. But in everything that I read, heard, and experienced since meeting Athman, they were purely and simply absent. They cast no shadows, their words had no resonance, their reflection in no way enlightened me. This break between my birth and childhood on the one hand and my faith on the other was so clear that it made me wonder where the reality of my existence was. Was I really born of a Muslim father and mother? How could I have remained so estranged from Islam, to the point of not finding any connection or obvious continuum between my birth and my desire for rebirth? I think history imposed a double fracture on me. A kind of exile squared . . .

I love my father, I love my mother, even though we spent our lives holding each other to the highest expectations.

For me, money was necessary for success, and for them, it was the end result that would confirm my success. We got so worn out from it that we forgot how to tell each other how much we loved each other. Thank goodness my mother never lost her habit of stroking my face in a gesture that felt like a true love poem. As for my father, he showed affection in his own way, standing in front of me, hands in his pockets, smiling as he said, "So, son . . ." before looking away after a few seconds. This silence was his poem.

I love my father and my mother, but we no longer had the words to express it.

Isn't the entire Koran one beautiful and magnificent language to tell God of our love? I think that if God dictated to us the language we are supposed to use in expressing our love to Him, it's because He knew that we didn't know how. Otherwise, He would have left us free to invent the language to love Him.

I mailed the letter but I'm not on the plane. Right now, I'm in a restaurant in front of a television screen that keeps showing the action over and over. The rapidity, precision, and acrobatics of the maneuver intensified the violence of the act to the extreme. Maybe that's the one divine aspect of it all—I'm really proud of my calculations. I saw people fainting around me, as if the shock physically assailed them. There is a power in national and community ties that makes people who are far away feel struck down by a crime which affects a nation or group. The panic around me was so great that I left the place. I felt out of place, I had the crazy feeling of being at a show that was over and the audience was clapping, and I was the only one wanting to yell out that the play was bad and that no one should be clapping. . . . I ran to the parking lot to get my car and rushed home to get out of there. People in the street were in a state of total disarray. I was afraid I wouldn't be able to find a way to get back home.

❊   ❊   ❊

No sooner had I closed the door behind me than I collapsed. I cried for a long time without understanding what I was crying about. I, who believed myself so clean, now came to feel suddenly cleansed and relieved. Could there be invisible dirt hidden within us? To get my bearings, I opened the Koran at random and read:

> "ALIF-LAM-RA (A.L.R.)
> "We have sent a Book down to you so that you may lead humans out of the shadows into the light with the permission of their Lord, to the path of Him who is worthy of consideration and praise.
> "God to whom belongs what is in the heavens and on the earth. Woe to the Repudiators for a merciless agony (which awaits them)!
> "We have sent a Messenger who speaks only in the language of his people so that he may explain things clearly to them. God leads astray whom He wants and guides whom He wants, and He is the Powerful and the Wise." (S14, V1–2–4)

The more I read, the less I could concentrate. . . . Was it because my tears were interfering with reading? I had the strange sensation that all of this water pouring out of me made me shrivel up like a disgusting dishrag, not even like the cotton that shrouds are made of. I had toiled for my rebirth and I had retreated in the face of God's desire. I didn't have enough confidence in the Hereafter. I hadn't desired death enough. I had not been sincere. I was hardened in sorrow, as if the souls of all of the dead came raining down on me like so many needles, contracting my muscles to the point of making me feel as if my bones were breaking. Or was it the tetanus of failure? I had no strength left in me to release the tension.

I got up to look for some food to appease the enormous hunger that accompanied this total upheaval. All that was left in the fridge was milk and dates. I ate a few without thinking. After the first gulp of milk, I immediately threw it all up, right down to the bile. I had its bitter taste in my mouth, and I couldn't feel my heart anymore. I couldn't tell whether it was still beating, or whether it had pulled away from all this turmoil, unaffected by gut wrenching crises which push away affection, feelings and tenderness. . . . I lay down on the bed to keep from fainting on my feet. My vision was blurry, my ears were ringing, and my knees were like rubber. Even a body knows not to stand up when it doesn't understand. Looking toward heaven at what was only a dirty ceiling, I tried to recite some verses I had learned:

After in the name of God . . .

But my memory remained silent. . . . I didn't know how anymore.

In the elevator leading from the parking lot to the departure area, Athman, slouched in a corner, had shot me an intense and piercing look of frightening determination. On the way out of the elevator, he brushed against my shoulder and said discreetly, "Did you take your pills?" I nodded yes, even though I hadn't. Throughout this entire process I had never acknowledged the presence of drugs. We had been under treatment for about a month. Pills to calm our nerves, capsules to enhance concentration and stimulate the intellect, others to relieve anxiety and fear. . . . Despite Atik's advice, I had stopped taking them because I was adamant about being fully conscious and acting with my own energy, strength, and emotion. I firmly believed that taking these pills would make me more into a mercenary than a soldier of God. One day when I raised the question with our guide, his answers didn't convince me:

"This is no ordinary act of faith, it's not like a prayer or Ramadan or a voyage to Mecca. This is an exceptional act of faith which falls under the exceptions as God defined them." He continued,

> "HE who rejected Allah after having believed in Him – with the exception of one restrained whose heart is imbued with the serenity of faith." (S16, V106)

I tried in vain to explain to him that I could never commit so important and dangerous an act if I were anything but a Muslim, and he answered me:

"For every limitation there is a solution. As long as you protect your intentions in practice, you will adjust your actions to allow your intentions to be expressed. That's why intentions and actions are not often in harmony. That's why Islam advocates peace. Only in the context of peace can the

acts of a Muslim be in harmony with intentions. In one of
the Hadith the Prophet says: 'Actions are only as valuable
as the intentions behind them.'"

I remained convinced, no matter what all the sheikhs said
to the contrary, that it was out of fear, energy, intelligence,
and natural inclination that such exploits should be carried
out, the value coming from the fact that ordinary people with
faith could reach beyond themselves. If I had exceptional
means available to me, it would be ridiculous for me not to
be exceptional. The guide didn't see it this way. For him, it
was like exposing yourself to unnecessary risks beyond your
control. Then he quoted an Arab proverb: "Force yourself
to make the effort, and God will help you." I answered that
the "God will help you" part was being replaced by capsules.
He was on the verge of anger, and explained to me:

"No, the pills are a part of your effort. You proved your
commitment to *ijtihad*, you went deep into yourself to uncover your weaknesses, your failings. That was your inner
discovery process. Then you found the material solution to
them. You made the effort to reduce your shortcomings, and
in so doing, you reduced the help of God. He who succeeds
in reducing the need for God's help makes more room for
God's love."

His view seemed to correspond to a kind of economy of
energy analysis, as if everything, even God's help, were quan-
tifiable. With this logic, the sheikh left the sphere of religion
and slipped into the political and military. This theory of "you
take away here so you can add there" had nothing to do with
religion and the divine. My skepticism about taking drugs
grew stronger, but I kept it to myself, all the more so because

the debate ended with the door closed on free choice: "Treatment is part of the 'action,' it is required."

In front of God and in body and soul, I had decided to be in charge of this decision. So I stopped taking the pills.

I had walked a few yards behind Athman in the airport concourse, because it was out of the question to be seen together. The way he walked, holding his back straight, told me that he would see this through to the end. His straight shoulders, his elegant gait, and perfectly balanced torso communicated a great air of self-confidence. He had an assured and decisive look about him. All of a sudden, it was the airport with its architecture that seemed fake and temporary to me. All of this aluminum, glass, and carpeting seemed thrown together in a makeshift way. The people seemed lost. Most of them had drawn faces due to their apprehension about taking a plane. In a matter of seconds, just as my eye caught sight of a cigarette butt smoldering in an ashtray, I asked myself for the first time in two months, "Why am I here?" This question scared me. I went to a soft drink machine to get a bottle of water to take my pills with. With a bottle of water in one hand and the pills in the other, I headed toward the trash bin saying to myself: "I'll decide over the trash bin."

For the last few months each second was a stage in life. As I reached the trash bin, I said to myself, "This is the moment of truth: either swallow them or toss them." I opened the bottle, took a drink, and the pills tumbled into the bottom of the trash bin just as the boarding for our flight was being announced. Omar had arrived. He was pale, his eyes wide, seemingly in control of the situation. I headed for the

men's room. I filled the sink and drowned my head in the
water. . . . With my shirt soaked to the waist, I left the
airport.

The next thing I knew, I was watching the action on the
television screen in the restaurant.

I was exhausted. I tried to recite the verses that I
learned—After in the name of God—but my memory was
silent. . . . I didn't know how anymore. . . .

I've often thought of committing suicide. This desire even
became common when I encountered severe mental and
physical deterioration and emotional emptiness. At such
moments, death seemed like the one and only immediate future available. The stupidest thing is that each time I would
conceive of it as a solution to my life. Suicide is always seen
as a solution to life by the person about to commit it. That's
precisely why suicide is a bad solution, because there's no life
after it. And you can't solve life's problems by doing away with
life. Only a suicidal person believes such a thing.

We accepted the same logic because we were the only
ones convinced that our death was a solution for God. But
to what extent would God accept our death for Him as the
one and only solution to our lives? Only God knows. So who
are we to dare to make such serious decisions for ourselves,
for Muslims, for humanity, for GOD?

Another thing I didn't really appreciate was the hoods.
When they said it was for security reasons, I didn't understand why. As far as I was concerned, we were each having to cope with our insecurity when we were separated,

but not when we were together. Being together is security, or else Islam and faith are not enough of a guarantee to make us feel secure in each other's presence with faces uncovered.

Five people joined together in Islam to give their lives for God in the name of Islam hooded for security reasons because no one was supposed to recognize the other—that's what I didn't understand. If there was a doubt of any sort, it would be a doubt about the faith of each of us. And if the planned operation is so dangerous as to require practices unknown to Islam in order to be carried out, it's that the action is not possible within Islam and that it can't claim to be a way to defend Islam. Piety prohibits us from using the same dirty weapons as the enemy and from resorting to intrigues and slander, for the Believers should be guided by their moral values at times of war as at times of peace, in wealth and in poverty.

But the guide persisted in explaining that covering our faces had nothing to do with doubting our integrity or our faith; it was a matter of putting a veil over our feelings. If fear or pain were seen on someone's face, the veil would keep from communicating it to the others. He said that the veil was common to Islam and to our customs, and not only to hide the beauty of women, but to protect men from the emotion that can arise from seeing fear in another. The hood in this specific instance is like a firebreak in the forest which can stop a fire from spreading, in case there is one.

So, what started out as a security measure—that means, if someone decides to talk he couldn't give names or physical descriptions—became an Islamic principle of protecting the faithful against the others' emotions which are, in effect, our own. So, I cover my face not to become afraid.

The responsibilities that were conferred on us came with greater and greater risks, both in terms of means and results. In order to shoulder them, we had to surrender ourselves more and more to God each day. I felt courage shrinking inside me. Each day I would scrape deeper into myself in search of humility like scraping the bottom of the well for a drop of water only to come up with mud. That's how I converted all of my fear into submission. But my fear was stronger, as if my submission to God had limitations while my fear was limitless. I had the extra fear of losing face in front of my companions and in front of God. I submitted myself to Him out of fear, but my fear was becoming greater, more infinite than God. Why didn't God feed my heart with enough courage? Why did He put me to the test of choosing what would be the destination of my prayers? What was I supposed to submit myself to? To Him, the Greatest, or to my fear?

I think that God helps us to improve our ways of making peace, of developing peace within us in a moderate way, but that He gives no help when it comes to excess. He is fundamentally against all extremes and immoderation.

The plan that they assigned us was excessive in every sense. What kind of Islam was supposed to help us manage this excess? No one could answer these questions except with the inaccessible greatness of God and His power. But in any case, everything that we were able to do was only a minuscule part of what He deserves from us.

During the final preparatory sessions, the rigor was so intense that no one even looked at each other. No complicity or solidarity was to be had. Although we were obviously a group, in reality, we were each separate from the others.

This solitude is also an Islamic principle which says that each individual is responsible for his actions before God. This independence of the individual in his faith had created an isolation within each of us in relation to God and for God. This gave rise to a feeling of mutual distrust among us, so that in the end we didn't move forward in solidarity but in the belief that each of us was useful to the others. So we had to keep an eye on each other and watch carefully because each was necessary for the action, and each would then stimulate the others to hold up under adversity and not out of solidarity. Complicity in adversity was more effective than solidarity. We went into war symbolically united, but we were really enemies because each of us spurred on the other to wish for death a bit more, just as we might serve up another drink not to contribute to the other's intoxication, but rather to our own.

Once this mechanism was in place, everything went along smoothly. At this point, all it took to keep us going to the end was a plan of such dimension and consequence that it could match the level of our exhilaration. . . .

My problem was not really whether to die or not to die, but rather how and why. For me, it wasn't about being God's suicide victim. To commit a crime against oneself in order to kill others, was that the kind of death that God accepts for His glory? If the innocence of the God that was sending us to death, as portrayed in our guide's sermons, greatly moved me, it didn't convince me.

But there is a logic in faith that troubles me: if God through His teachings can send us to death in order to avenge the Muslim *Ummah* plunged into poverty, and if faith can convince us to die, why can't it convince us to accept poverty, since death and poverty are the will of God? And if some say that poverty is our responsibility in the Here and Now, why then fight to go to the Hereafter as a way of solving problems in the Here and Now? If the problems of Muslims are caused by their religion, then God and no one else should be asked for help. And if their problems in the Here and Now are due to their own fault, why mix God up in all of it?

And if the problem for Muslims is the heathens, the solution could only be political and not religious because in religion the punishment of heathens falls to God, not to us. Theologically speaking, no one can ever be a substitute for God. God created the devil so that we would believe in His existence, but if we decided to get rid of all devils so as not to be threatened in our faith, we would be eliminating a fundamental element of our faith since it requires us to believe in the existence of devils.

We must strengthen our faith in order to solve problems in the theological context in which they appear. The Here and Now and the Hereafter are two places within a single religion but our theological responsibility is different depending on the place. In the Here and Now we are responsible for ourselves in the face of God, especially for how we understand

God's message. The Hereafter is God's space where He places all of humanity to face the last judgment. If, as faithful Believers, we defy the limits of the space of our faith, that proves that we have lost all sense of limits. In such a case, how can we claim to be inscribed within the limits of true Guidance?

From a certain time on, I felt carried away by something other than religion. The spiritual journey was only the first stage of a process that changed course toward something that ignored everything but its own success.

We started off as Muslims to redress the humiliation of Muslims, and then little by little we turned into Islamic cowboys acting under the pretext of attacking those who were portrayed as cowboys. I had the clear impression that as soon as we moved into the action phase we stopped being Muslims. When we acted, everything was allowed. "Necessity makes for law" and "Intention makes for faith" were the only Islamic laws that were applied to the action.

I'm exhausted. I'm still trying to recite the verses I had learned.

After in the name of God . . .

My memory is still silent. I don't know anymore. I think that Islam is in the same state on the planet. After the name of God, memory stops . . . and each person speaks in his own way. Each person fills this silence with personal anguish, fears, and revenge. On the day when this memory speaks again, Islam will find its way toward better paths. Actually, that was what I wanted in choosing to be reborn. . . .

I'm stopping my writing here. I think the police have come to arrest me . . . I'm sure of it.

❀   ❀   ❀

After three days of nonstop interrogation, I was taken to see someone in the visiting area. I was sure it was my mother. Who else could possibly come to see me? Given what had happened, it couldn't be Jamal.

When I walked inside, to my great surprise, I found Jenny waiting. She was deathly pale, her features frozen in the middle of her face. She moved slowly toward the security glass, and with no sign of emotion or affection, she announced in a calm voice that belied her seething anger:

"I'm here because your mother asked me to come before she died."

"When? How? Where?"

"She left her treatment a week ago because she didn't feel well. Dr. Houry had her hospitalized. She tried to contact you but you couldn't be reached. She ended up calling me when she saw your photo shown on television — because you were the only one on the passenger list who didn't get on the plane. She asked me if I knew anything. I said I hadn't heard from you in over two months. The next morning around nine I went to see her. Dr. Houry told me of her death and that she had left a letter for you."

"When did this all happen?"

"The day after your arrest. The nurses who arrived on the early shift found her dead with the letter in one hand and a pen in the other. She'll be buried tomorrow with your father."

She slipped me the letter through the slot and added, "As for me, I don't understand, and I'll never understand! Goodbye forever."

She left the room in tears, bent over in pain, without giving me a chance to even ask her about Keytal. I was taken back to my cell in the solitary confinement block. I stripped naked in my cell and read my mother's letter illuminated by the narrow ray of light that passed through the tiny opening in the door.

Raouf, my son, my only child . . .
    God forgive me.
    Your father in the cemetery, you I don't know where, and me left staring at your father's lute and your graduation picture. Is that what America boils down to for me? My son, didn't you understand that by killing yourself, you are killing your mother? Did you think that maybe God wouldn't let me die even if He welcomed your death with the generosity that He awards to the martyrs?
    My son, your father and I became exiles so that you might have a happy life. We didn't dream of the States for ourselves but for you. If you attack our dream you reduce our life here to nothing. Have we failed so miserably?
    My son, my only child . . .
    The building you attacked is much more solid than your mother, and it crumbled before the eyes of the world. As for me, an exile in every sense, I'm crumbling stone by stone, alone and neglected. Your act is insane because it is consistent with nothing, it's so loud that it says nothing. It is so criminal that it's totally unjust, it's so grandiose that it's surreal, almost virtual, just like your faith. You have the illusion of doing this for God.

My son, they made your virtual view of the world seem possible so that they could instill hatred in the name of God, but the misfortune of your acts is real. My only child, what's going to become of you? Recently, I don't know what modesty is anymore or the limit of my self-control. . . . But, I must tell you that even though I went through menopause several years ago, I've been bleeding profusely since this afternoon. I didn't mention it to Dr. Houry. I feel as if I'm having a miscarriage, or else all of the bad blood that I've been holding in over the years has decided to wash me away. I'm afraid to cry for fear of drying up instantaneously. I would like to finish this letter but I don't know where it will end.

My son, you, my only son . . . whenever I pronounce the word "love" L.O.V.E., there has never been anyone but you in my mind. I loved my mother, my father, my brothers, my sisters, and your father with a love already defined by tradition. My mother dictated how I was to love her and my father. With my brothers and sisters, we figured out how to love each other in a way not displeasing to our parents. Your father loved this upbringing in me, and being a prisoner of this upbringing, I loved him.

My son, my only child, you are the only one that I loved freely. I created the freedom to love in order to love you, in the hope that this would allow you to be the freest man in the world. Does freedom lead to such perdition? I sensed that you were changing but I thought it was more related to your separation from Jenny than to your repentance. My son, did you repent just to commit such an enormous sin? I don't understand anything anymore. . . . In spite of all of the intelligence I invented for you, to be capable of giving you the best upbringing, I don't understand, and at this point, I feel illiterate.

I can't drink a glass of water because my stomach rejects it. My body refuses to take in food. It pushes on my insides and shatters them.

Maybe I'm in the process of disintegrating from the inside. If this continues, I'll end up a hollow carcass, a skeleton covered with its skin ready to be mummified in its misfortune for eternity.

I feel all of the changes that a woman's body feels in the beginning of a pregnancy as it gets ready for a baby, except that in me they are occurring in a vacuum. The baby is not there, and this absence compounds the pain suffered by each function of the woman's body. This absence is catastrophic for a mother, for a father. You should know, my son, that thousands of women at this very moment, as I write, are suffering as I suffer. Don't they also have a God? Even if they don't, their sorrow will invent one. I think of them and I cry for my pain all the more for having been put in the position of being seen as their enemy. . . .

This God that you fight for is also mine. No one has the right to use a religion practiced by millions throughout the world for personal reasons and to claim the faith of all the others. Especially in Islam, where it's obvious that any action taken on behalf of the collective interest, if there is such an interest, can only be decided collectively, unless the one who acts is the Prophet brought back to life. Then someone should explain to us when, where, and how he reappeared, and we'll organize a pilgrimage to see him.

My son, where is your pain? Did I love you wrong? Did I inadvertently ooze hatred thinking that I was giving love? Or did I, in keeping with my professional training, modify your emotional genetics and create an organism resistant to love? The absurdity of my questions is as enormous as the absurdity of your group's act. What troubles me, what eats away at me, what will end up killing me is not understanding how you could have stowed away in my womb. Not telling me about things in your life is normal, you're on your own and I don't expect to know everything. But to hide yourself from me, dissembling in my presence to keep me from knowing—that I find intolerable, because that means that whether consciously or unconsciously you put me in the same category as your victims. What did I do to deserve this? Did exile lead us astray to the point that a mother is no longer a mother, a son no longer a son, and God is an organizer of terrorist attacks?

I wish I could hear your voice now. Then I would try to figure out the sense of what you say, not by the meaning of the words, but by the smell of your breath, by the dryness of your throat, by the heaviness of your tongue and by the way your lips move. I would try to hear you from within my womb, and even if I were bleeding, it wouldn't matter just as long as I could understand. It was from me that you came! For my whole life, and in spite of me, you determine my health or my sickness. Up until now, you've been to a large extent the source of my happiness. At least tell me it wasn't faked, that it was the simple, everyday happiness of an ordinary mother.

Oh, my son, if you only knew. Now that I think back, oh, how I love the simple everyday moments even more. The

exceptional situations are the ones that hurt. Whether
they're glorious or unhappy, they hurt me, and you pushed
me to the limit of exceptional misfortune. Everything got
worse because of my lack of comprehension. Not understanding is the front door to death. What is it that you don't
understand, that pushes you toward a death that kills others, a death outside of the human?

A drop of blood just fell from my nose . . . I don't know
if that's an important sign. In our culture, when a woman
bleeds from her vagina, it's normal, even when it's abnormal,
because a primary function of this organ is to bleed. I think
it's my sinuses in the best case, or my brain in the worst. I
don't feel dizzy at the moment, which is a good sign, but I
won't talk anymore about my physical state in this letter, so
I can try to say the most important things I have to tell you.

My son, I'm your mother so that one day you could be
my father. I accompanied you into life so that you could accompany me on my way to death. That's peace, that's life,
that's joy. By choosing to die violently in the name of God,
by leaving me alone in my family and rejected by society,
how could you believe in a faith that leaves me like this? To
reach God, we need a chain and I am a link in that chain.
Even if your death earns me Paradise, you leave me to wait
in the worst of hells in the meantime.

How could you have ignored me like that? Did they
instill in you such a hatred of women that you saw me as
the source of your weaknesses, even though I had for so long
been your only strength?

Islam cannot be defended viscerally since it is the very
teaching of peace, and yet, the Prophet said to us: "*Whoever*

puts an end to his anger will be protected by God from the punish-ment of hell."

Did our history transform us into savages? Did we repeatedly suppress and acculturate ourselves to the extent that we no longer know how to read our religion? Have we gone back to the caves and the caveman mentality? Certainly Muhammad had his revelation of the Koran in a cave, but does that make us all Muhammads? It's no reason to think that anyone who lives in a cave becomes the Prophet. Perhaps history repeats itself, but religion does not, it perpetuates itself, and that doesn't mean repeating the same wars.

No God could preach death to the faithful, because He needs them down here if He is to exist on high. And when our people don't serve as models, who then will help to reunite us with our God and our faith? God gave us Islam so that we might lead exemplary lives, not for us to orchestrate exemplary deaths. Let us live what God gives us and let Him determine the exemplary punishment. No one is more capable than He.

One can't defend Islam by using practices which do not draw from the essence, philosophy and convictions of Islam. Never has a religion been more defended against itself than Islam.

Could Muslim society be afraid of accumulating knowledge? Or does it favor the art of cultivating ignorance in order to keep us as fetuses in God's womb forever? Are we capable of becoming adult Muslims? Would God accept us as adults? We are children who want nothing to do with the world. The proof is that it's our children

who initiate wars; they throw stones and turn themselves
into bombs. The reason is that Islam has become so child-
ish that it is the children who now understand it best. And
when the adults try to figure things out, they don't do any
better.

As for Jamal, maybe God finds nothing wrong with
him. But Jamal knows nothing about the problems of the
devout workers—those who work to have the dignity to
pray, and pray not to lose their jobs. All of these quiet,
hardworking Muslims need God for their everyday life.
These believers work from morning until night and confront
Satan countless times without even noticing because they
are swept away by the torrent of poverty. These Muslims
are so ashamed to ask much of God that they would never
dare to ask him to attack the U.S.; they already have enormous difficulty asking Him to guarantee them a decent living. You have to have the arrogance and insensitivity of a
rich person to ask God for help with such attacks. The poor
have enough trouble just drawing the attention of God to
their suffering because they feel guilty about not knowing
how to read the Koran properly. When they come home
exhausted after a long day's work, they can't think about
prayer, and they end up losing the habit of praying, and then
the memory of it. . . . They meet at the bar where they rub
elbows and down beers trying to quench a different kind of
thirst. With childlike innocence, they ask God what He's
done with their prayers, and then realize they're drunk. So,
overcome with guilt, they ask God for forgiveness as they
head home, having nothing in their culture to explain their

madness. They fall asleep whispering to their drunkenness, "You made me drink bitterness. I'll complain to God. . . ." Jamal doesn't go to sleep in the same throes of pain as those Muslims.

I'm not an imam, a theologian, or a professor of Islamic studies. I'm just a woman who found Islam at the center of my life at birth. In my exile, it's been at the center of my thinking, and in my history it's been at the center of my internal and external contradictions. Islam was the bright light of the joyful feasts of my childhood, it was the heartbreak of my adolescence, the exile of my adulthood, and the pain of my life as a woman. I was taught, even before puberty, that above all else I was responsible for two things in my life: my own life, because "it is God who gives life and only He can take it away," and my faith, because "it is through our faith that God will recognize us." I was taught that we had to cultivate our faith in life because it would redeem our death. And to redeem our death was to save our soul.

Putting this into equation form is instructive in that it allows us to identify the separate terms of another equation: the one designed to make me a victim. My life is worthless because my faith is worthless, therefore my soul is worthless, so killing me amounts to killing nothing. In the name of what? In the name of God.

While we are taught that after a few weeks the fetus has a soul and that's why abortion is forbidden by God, how can we accept the aborting of the children of entire societies in the name of God?

My exile led me to ask another question that would occur naturally to any intelligent person in my situation: without repudiating my father and my mother should I exile myself from my faith in order to save my soul?

Before God, these are the cruel questions which I face when circumstances become violent and unbearable. The answers can only be as absurd.

These same questions are being asked in the Muslim world today. But it rejects the absurdity of the answers, it doesn't want to face up to them, and tries to reconcile them.

Is Islam compatible with socialism?

Is Islam compatible with capitalism?

Is Islam compatible with today's modern world?

But we all know that Islam, like every other religion, is compatible only with itself. In everything else, religions negotiate.

Ever since my earliest childhood days, I've heard only one kind of controversy about Islam, and all discussion is brought to a sudden halt by the same type of answers:

"Islam liberated women, but Muslims repressed them."

"Through the *shura* Islam instituted a system of cooperation and exchange better than democracy. But after our leaders proclaimed Islam the state religion, they repressed the people."

"Islam has a conception of economy and financial principles that reduces poverty and limits personal wealth. But it is the Muslims corrupted by Western political views who prefer to impose 'interest' in order to serve their own interests."

In other words, Islam is perfect and it's the Muslims who are imperfect.

If Islam is perfect to the point that each Muslim can only be imperfect, it takes away from its faithful any chance of being good believers. Or else, perfection in Islam is super-human and no human being can hope to attain it fully. Is Islam attainable? Is it of an inhuman transcendence?

I grew up in Islam with the idea of a religion too great, too perfect. It was taught to me by believers who never stopped telling me about their own powerlessness, hoping to teach me humility. In what and in whom should we be-lieve? In the greatness of God? In the weakness of his faith-ful? In the unbelievers' hatred? This triple mentality dictates three ways of loving God that I never managed to bring together in a single love. Without *tawhiḍ*, I am no longer Muslim because the oneness of God is inscribed into the oneness of the love that one can have for Him because He is One.

All Muslims teach that Islam is greater, more complete and perfect than Christianity and Judaism, and that the Koran is the *khatam* of religions. When I was a child, I used to think that before getting to the Koran, it would be logi-cal to first become Jewish and then Christian before dar-ing to hope to become Muslim. From my way of thinking like a schoolgirl, in order to reach senior year, you had to first pass through sophomore and junior year. At that point, my grandmother explained to me that one shouldn't soil oneself with the other religions, because the purity of Islam was to be protected. With that, a more serious concern over-took me, and I asked her,

"Do we believe in the other Books or not?"

"We believe in the existence of the other Books, but not in the religions that they set forth."

"So, we believe in the Books, but not in what they say? And if we don't believe what's said in a Book, what is left in the Book that we do believe in?"

"That the Books exist, that's for sure. But as Muslims, we have our own opinion of what they say. Their Books are false and incomplete."

"In the end, Grandma, the Books exist for us, but they don't say the same thing for us as they say for them. So, we don't believe in what they believe."

"That's it, my child. . . . That's it."

"So then why do you tell us that we believe in the other Books?"

"The Hebrew religion and the Christian one are taught to us by God in the Koran. Yes, we believe in the other Books, but strictly according to our Book."

So I understood that if there were atheist Jews it was because the Torah was incomplete, and that was normal. If there were atheist Christians, it was because Christianity was flawed. But that there couldn't be atheist Muslims because Islam was so perfect and definitive that anyone who knew Islam couldn't become an atheist without becoming the devil personified.

Our elders thought that by inflating the image of God, they were going to elevate the religion itself. To make us afraid, they taught us the opposite of reality.

The process of accumulating so many confusing ideas just to understand the basic premises of religion begins when

we are children. Then, as adults, swimming in all kinds of
contradictions, we try to understand our society, and we feel
pushed at every moment of our lives to redefine our religious
identity and to reexamine the spirit and content of our faith.
Because faith is not a given.

In a natural and human way, I had to put my faith in
life in order to save my life, in serenity in order to control
my fear, and in peace in order to reduce violence. Everything had to be taken care of through my will, in relation to
my desire through the tears of my insomnia.

When I tried to put my situation into words, the only
word that I could come up with was "conflict." I am in conflict with myself, and that's infernal. What can I do? I am
not as lucky as a lot of Muslims. God didn't resolve all of
the problems for me even though I try to do everything in
my power not to be a problem for God myself.

My son, my only child,

I want to tell you that until now I have lived through
two wars and, at every stage of my thinking, a number of
exiles. I tried not to stray, but I lost my way several times.
And each time, I found a different "me." At the end of this
wandering, like that of Moses, like the suffering of Jesus,
and like the solitude of Muhammad, I encountered only
myself. If my journey is made with no promise of a promised land, and my crucifixion with no promise of resurrection and without visits from angels in my cave, that proves
that I am only a woman.

At the end of my perdition, I'm convinced that the space
of peace can be built within a human space, where man will

have learned on his own how to respect others based on his own experience and not within the space of religions.

If I left the straight path, it's because my heartbreak pulled me onto the footpaths of human pain. Obviously, I'm not making the same journey. The straight path is a series of questions that find their answers in the Book. But my son, when life questions me and the Book doesn't answer, prayer loses its meaning for me, anguish prevents me from simply submitting. And I find myself all alone. . . .

That's why I need clear markers which rise up in me, like the steam of a bath, a warm hand, a sparkling lift in life's destiny which alone has the magic to determine who is my brother.

Why is this so painful for me to say?

My son, if God is also this pain then I think I have the faith and you can be sure of yours. But your mother says to you: this pain is not acknowledged by God. That's why your mother will never be a prophetess.

Modernity is not a clear path to follow; it's a direction you take. It's not a technology you purchase, but the values you adopt and a legal framework that you construct. In a word, modernity is a state of mind above all which develops out of constant improvements in the cultural level of societies.

In the face of modernity, our leaders are nervous, unsure. Because, on the one hand, they're fascinated by the technical and logistical possibilities that it offers, but on the other, they're afraid of the values that it creates. In other words, our nations do all they can to acquire modern technology, but they refuse to let their people live in the context of modern-day values.

If, in addition to the inconsistency of our countries' leadership, we add the arrogance of countries which epitomize modernity, and if these countries flaunt their superiority and subject others to its domination, then that will push even those countries which aspire to modernity to seek refuge in tradition and to pump up the deflated culture that defines them, as their way of taking a stand against the all-powerful forces of modernity.

The international community must use all of its influence to ensure that the means of modernity benefit the people rather than reinforce the tyranny of the powers that be. Because if peoples today seem weaker than in the past, it's because the instruments of tyranny are a thousand times more effective. Consciously or unconsciously, people today, even the most fundamentalist among them, desire modernity, and the most violent ones express this desire through violence.

You must not forget that the majority of nations, underdeveloped because their leaders have been so corrupt, have known very little of modernity. All they've seen from the developed countries is the modernity that comes with waves of tourists who flaunt themselves shamelessly, enjoying the climate and natural beauty, while those who live there can't even afford medication.

These nations, more than any others, know that the solution to their problems is in modernity. What they don't understand is the reasons that prevent them from having it. Is it because of their own incompetent leaders or because those who control modernity refuse to share it? Because the question that plagues them is not "to be or not to be modern" but "why can't we achieve modernity"?

The unfortunate part is that in producing answers to this question, we end up creating a culture of despair, to which religious fanaticism is only one response among many others. As a result of this fascination that the image of modernity exerts on the peoples who aspire to it, an image that links sex to power, fundamentalism provides an easy antidote. For sex, there is the veil; for human power, there is the power of God.

But the actions that result from this are necessarily absurd and irrational in the way they are carried out, in their choice of target, their reach, and their objective.

The modern world which is defined by rationality can prevail only through rational means. If it has to incorporate irrational behavior just to take control of the situation, one can only wish it much luck, for the solution is not to fight violence, but to eradicate the causes that created the violence in the first place.

My son! I feel at the end. . . . I can't write anymore, my vision . . . is failing . . .

    Your

    Mo . . .

Glossary of Terms

Abu: father of; for example, "Abu-Raouf" means "father of Raouf." In Arab culture, at the birth of a child, the father takes the first name of the son or daughter preceded by the prefix "abu." This is done, among other reasons, to protect the descendant and especially to affirm the recognition of the child by the father.

Al-Anfal: "The Spoils," title of the eighth sura of the Koran

Al-Isha: evening prayer; the last of the day

Al-Tawbah: Return to God or The Repentance, title of the ninth sura of the Koran

Allahu Akbar: God is great

As-salaam alaikum: peace be with you

Ansar: supporters who greeted the Prophet at his arrival in Medina after his exile from Mecca where he received death threats from all of the Meccan tribes

Astaghfir Allah: pardon to God

Babour: boat

Baraka: blessing or spiritual power

Baroud: gunpowder

Barzakh or *isthmus:* barrier impossible to cross except by God's will; an in-between point, between life and death

Buraq: winged horse of the Prophet

Dawah: preaching or sermon

Du'a: prayer

Eid al-Adha or *Id al-Adha:* the Great Feast during which Muslims slit the throat of a lamb in commemoration of the sacrifice of Abraham. The word *Eid* or *Id* means a religious feast or celebration.

Fatiha: The Opening, title of the first sura of the Koran

Fatwa: a religious opinion handed down from the most important imam of a community, a country, or a sect. It is not a law, but a powerful directive for the events experienced within the community for which it is issued.

Gandura: traditional garb similar to a djellaba

Hadith: words and sayings attributed to the Prophet and which constitute a secondary legal reference after the Koran

Halal: what is allowed by God

Hamza: refers to Muhammad's paternal uncle, a convert and brave warrior of Islam

Haram: the opposite of *halal* or that which God forbids

Houris: celestial beings of the female sex "promised" to good Muslims when they enter Paradise

Ijtihad: a continual effort toward deeper interpretation of the precepts of Islam

Jahilites: the uninitiated; a word for men before the advent of Islam in the pre-Islamic period known as the era of "ignorance" or of *jahiliyya*

Jihad: holy war; may also be considered as a personal "combat" within the self; in a broader context a "striving" to be in accord with God

Jinn: spirits; demons

Kaaba: a black cube-shaped structure; the most sacred shrine of Islam which Muslims face during prayer; see *Mihrab*

Khatam: has two meanings: "that which concludes" or "a closing" or a "seal"

Khouchou: position of prostration and submission to God during prayer

Kafir (sing); *Kufar* (pl.): anyone who commits a sinful act; also applies to all non-Muslims

Mamluk: slave; refers in this case to freed white slaves who took power in Egypt and Syria around 1250

Mihrab: an ornamental arch set into the wall of a mosque from which the imam leads prayer. Facing Mecca, where the Kaaba is located, the mihrab marks the spiritual direction toward which each Muslim addresses his daily prayers.

Moubaya'a: allegiance

Salaf: see *Ummah al-Salaf*

Sharia: body of Islamic laws which define the path to be followed by all Muslims (legal code)

Shaytan: devil

Shura: religious consultation

Taghut: name of a pagan divinity mentioned several times in the Koran

Tahara: purity

Tawhid: unification; belief in the oneness of God

Ulama: men of knowledge; wise men

Ummah al-Salaf: the community of Salafists, fundamentalist elders of Medina who advocated the universal application of Muslim rules in accordance with those practiced by Muslims living in Medina at the time of the Prophet

Ummah Islamiyya: the community of Muslim believers

Yaqin: conviction; certainty

Glossary of Key Figures

Abd as-Samad: contemporary reciter of the Koran, of Egyptian origin

Abu Bakr: first companion of the Prophet and the first caliph after the Prophet's death

Abu Sa'id al-Khudari: companion of Muhammad

Abu Sufyan: powerful leader of Mecca and the Quraysh tribe

Abu Talib al-Makki: (d. 990) early religious thinker, author of "Nourishment of Hearts"

Aisha: favorite wife of the Prophet, called the "mother of Muslims."

Ali ibn Abi Talib: cousin of the Prophet

Ali ibn Sahl: (d. 870) scholar physician, author of first medical encyclopedia

Hasan ibn Ali: grandson of the Prophet

Hudhayfa: companion of Muhammad

Ibn al Qayyim al-Jawziyya: born in Damacus in 1292, a disciple of Ibn Taymiyya, he wrote *The Soul's Journey after Death* among other works.

Ibn Taymiyya: Syrian theologian, died in 1328. Disciple of Ibn Hanbal, founder of one of the four Sunni law schools in the ninth century, he was the teacher of Abd al-Wahhab, founder of Wahhabism.

Jamal al-Din al-Afghani: (d. 1897) Afghan thinker; first reformer who sought a renaissance of Islam

Khalid ibn al-Walid: military leader and loyal companion of the Prophet

Omar ibn al-Khattab: companion of the Prophet who became the second caliph after the death of the Prophet. He was assassinated in a mosque while praying.

Quraysh: name of the tribe into which the Prophet was born

Salah al-Din al-Ayubi (Saladin): imam and Syrian military leader who conquered the Crusaders of Richard the Lionheart

Sheikh Abu al-Darda: companion of Muhammad

Sheikh Muhammad Mitwali al-Shaarawi: born in Egypt in 1911; after completing his studies at the Islamic university El Azhar in Cairo in 1943, he became a professor in the same university. In 1976 he was named minister of religious affairs and in 1980 became a member of the Islamic Research Academy.

Sidna Aïssa: Jesus